Ebenezer Pemberton

The world's furniture

A Novel. Vol. 3

Ebenezer Pemberton

The world's furniture
A Novel. Vol. 3

ISBN/EAN: 9783337273521

Printed in Europe, USA, Canada, Australia, Japan

Cover: Foto ©Andreas Hilbeck / pixelio.de

More available books at **www.hansebooks.com**

THE

WORLD'S FURNITURE.

A NOVEL.

"Man's love is of man's life a thing apart ;
'Tis woman's whole existence. . . . . ."
BYRON.

IN THREE VOLUMES.

VOL. III.

LONDON:

CHARLES J. SKEET, PUBLISHER,

10, KING WILLIAM STREET,

CHARING CROSS.

1861.

LONDON :
Printed by A. Schulze, 13, Poland Street.

WORLD'S FURNITURE

CHAPTER I.

WHEN luncheon was over the next day, and Mrs. Chichester had not come, Lady Fordyce, according to her promise, drove over to her. She left Hilda at home, as she knew it was about her, her mother desired to talk. Poor Mrs. Chichester felt quite nervous at the task before her; she could not feel so warmly on the subject as Arthur had done, but she had done what he had

desired—first watched Hilda and Walter
Wentworth, but she saw nothing to notice;
she then spoke to Wentworth, and felt all
the time as if she was doing a very improper
thing, and a very useless one.   Lastly, she
was going to speak to her sister-in-law.

Lady Fordyce determined she would not
appear to be at all conscious of the cause
of Mrs. Chichester's request to see her, and
so poor Rose met with no help.   She was
sitting at her usual place at the little
table by the window, employed at some in-
comprehensible-looking work, for it must
have been equally incomprehensible to herself, for nothing ever was to be shown for all
the hours she seemed employed.

" Why did you not come and lunch with
us, Rose, as you half-promised ? you can't
tell me you were not well enough, for your
looks would belie your words."

" No, Mary, I will tell you the truth.   I
felt like a child putting off, as long as pos-

sible, taking a disagreeable medicine," replied Rose, smiling.

"That is not complimentary. Am I the disagreeable medicine?"

"You know better than that; but what I am obliged to say to you is—don't you know what it is?"

"How should I? Nothing wrong with Arthur, I hope?"

There was a little feeling of annoyance in Lady Fordyce's breast, that Mrs. Chichester should interfere with Hilda in any way. She thought she had no right to do so. It was quite true, as her mother, the world would say she had; but she had been so little with her, knew so little of her, that it, under her circumstances, was a different thing.

"No, Arthur is going on very well; yet he is principally the cause of my wishing to see you. It is by his desire, or rather, his wish—of course he, as a young man going out a great deal and hearing everything people say, can judge better than I can who rarely move out, and still more rarely see people."

"Can judge better of what, Rose? Pray tell me at once what it is, and if it is anything I can help you in, you know how glad I shall be."

Lady Fordyce spoke rather irritably, which did not tend to make Mrs. Chichester more at ease.

"You must not be angry with me, Mary, if I say anything that annoys you," and she laid her hand on Lady Fordyce's arm, and spoke in a conciliating tone. "Believe me I see no necessity for saying anything; but Arthur, who is very tenacious of the world and its ways, thinks otherwise. He thinks that Hilda, considering her engagement to David, is too much taken up with Mr. Wentworth's attentions to her, and that people remark it, though we may not."

She could not bring herself to say all her

son had told her, and she tried to put what she did say in as mild a form as possible; she paused there, however, only from the sudden change that took place in her sister-in-law's face. She seemed as if some dreadful vision was before her; her eyes were fixed, and staring as if she were grappling with some invisible enemy, but it was but for a moment; and in her answer, no one would have thought that anything unusual had been said.

"How foolish of Arthur! Does he not think I and your brother are enough to guard Hilda from the world's evil tongue? Tell him, from me, not to fill his head with foolish notions, there are quite enough real troubles in the world without conjuring up imaginary ones."

"Then you don't think Hilda likes Mr. Wentworth?" asked Rose, rather anxiously.

"What nonsense, my dear Rose! Is she not going to marry David?"

Poor Lady Fordyce, she said it to reassure and comfort the mother, and keep herself up too; but she failed in both cases completely, as neither of them thought so, for Rose thought only her sister-in-law was mistaken, not herself; and Lady Fordyce felt she had not deceived herself, but she hoped she had Rose.

Well, after all, women are not so selfish, even towards each other. They are jealous of one another very often—indeed, almost always; but if sorrow or trouble befall those that are, perhaps, their greatest rivals, the woman will forget herself and her jealousies in the grief she may, perhaps, find it in her power to assuage, or, at all events, share.

Lady Fordyce and Mrs. Chichester had no cause to be rivals or jealous of each other. Hilda, of course, was their only stumbling-block. Lady Fordyce knew that she was dearer to her niece than, at all events, any other woman. Mrs. Chichester knew that her greatest hope had been, when she first resigned all care of her child over to her sister-in-law, that Hilda might love her more dearly than she had loved herself. It had been an unselfish hope, as it was for the child's sake only, and she certainly had gained her desire; for though Hilda was very fond of her mother, she did not feel for her that love that she felt for her aunt, Lady Fordyce; and Mrs. Chichester both felt it would be safer and wiser to say no more on the subject.

Rose had done what she was compelled to do; Lady Fordyce had done what she had been requested to do, and that was enough. But what had been gained by it? Absolutely nothing. Lady Fordyce had her eyes opened, it is true, as to what was the cause of Hilda's conversation with her yesterday, but it only added to her dilemma. Before she had only a phantom to deal with, now it was a real man of flesh and blood.

When Lady Fordyce got into her carriage,
she gave the order, " To Mrs. Graham's."
It was a sudden thought, but she often acted
on impulse, and frequently found it the best
and wisest.   She began to hope, as she approached their house, that she should find
them out.   She began to dread the interview, because when it occurred to her to
go, she determined to speak only on the
subject with Mrs. Graham, and now she
wished herself out of it ; but it was not to
be.   The servant knew, without being told,
that his mistress would get out if they were
at home : and so, when the door was opened,
and the footman came and opened the carriage door, she had nothing for it but to get
out.   She found all at home ; father, mother,
and son.

" You are just the person we want," said
Mrs. Graham, as Lady Fordyce walked in.
" Come and help me to persuade David to

agree to a little plan of his father's and mine."

"I'm sure David won't be persuaded by a woman in anything, will you, David?" said Lady Fordyce.

"Yes, if it were reasonable; but it isn't; and I am sure you will take my side," replied David.

"But what is the proposition you won't give into?" asked Lady Fordyce.

"Only—" began Mr. Graham, but his son interrupted him.

"Let me answer my own questions, father. It is this, Lady Fordyce. They want to get up some private theatricals, and for Hilda and I to be the heroes in the piece."

"That's not the way to put it, dear David; of course, that sounds odd. There is a little piece that Mrs. Phillips was telling me of—I can't remember the name of it— but she said the hero's part would just do for David, and the heroine's for Hilda; and she

said it would be so nice to have some theatricals, for one scarcely ever sees amateur
performances now."

" The piece is called ' The Deceived One,'"
said Mr. Graham, half-afraid of speaking
after his son's putting him down.

" And my daughter proposed your having
it acted here?" asked Lady Fordyce.

" Yes," said Mrs. Graham ; " she has just
left us.   It was only to-day she spoke of it,
but David won't hear of it."

" I think David is right," said Lady Fordyce, quietly; " it would place both himself
and Hilda in a false position.   If their marriage is to be made known to the world, let
it be done in a proper manner, but not by
acting their parts in a farce; it would lead
to much talking and ill-natured remarks ;
and people would think they could have no
serious thought of marriage were they to do
such a thing."

Poor Mrs. Graham was very disappointed,

she thought Lady Fordyce would be sure to second what Mrs. Phillips had proposed, whereas, it had precisely the contrary effect. It was quite enough that it was Matilda's suggestion for her to feel quite sure there was some mischief intended. She now recollected, too, one or two little hints her daughter had dropped, that made her suspect Matilda knew more about Hilda than she fancied, and, probably, had remarked what she never had done, her attachment to Mr. Wentworth.

It had the effect of preventing Lady Fordyce saying anything this time to the Grahams, as she had intended to do. What she had really decided, in the few moments it took her to go up-stairs, was, to have asked Mrs. Graham when she thought the young people's marriage had better take place, but now she would leave it for a few days. Not that there really was the least excuse why she should not now, as well as before the theatricals were proposed, but she made use of them as a plausible excuse, and thought it one—at the time.

It was not till she was comfortably leaning back in her carriage, driving home, that she bethought herself that, really, one thing was totally irrelevant of the others.

Hilda had not forgotten to send her invitation to Mary Fenton, and so some part of the time of her aunt's absence had been spent in writing her a long letter, asking her to come up as soon as her mother would allow her, and giving her short details of her gaieties.

She did not mention Arthur's name, she was not sure whether it might not strike Mrs. Fenton as strange that Mary should be invited; if his name were mentioned, it might help her to solve the cause.

How true it is conscience makes cowards of us all. Did Hilda not feel she had a motive of her own for inviting Mary, it

never would have struck her that Mrs. Fenton would attribute the invitation to any
other than her wish to see Mary, and give
her a little amusement in London, knowing
that they never went to town themselves,
and the country rarely had much dissipation
going on.

When her letter was finished, she sent it
to the post, and went and put on her bonnet,
and taking "Madelaine," a pretty, simple
French story, in her hand, took the key of
the Apsley Gardens, and walked in by the
gate just opposite their house. She intended
to read to avoid thinking; she had found the
latter such a useless and worrying employ-
ment, that anything was better.

There is a seat, not far from the gate,
quite hidden by shrubs and trees, and on
that seat Hilda sat down, as she could see no
one, and, she thought, not be seen; but in
that she was mistaken, for there was a small
opening at the side which showed a few of

the iron bars that railed in the gardens, and if any one chanced to be passing, and happened to look, they would have seen Hilda's pretty profile, like a picture with a frame of flowers and leaves.

But she was quite unconscious of this, so she made herself as comfortable as she could, and opened her book, determined to read very steadily.

She might have been so about an hour, when she heard a more than usual amount of noise, a rushing of horses, a multitude of human voices, shouting, screaming, and calling out every description of opposite orders. " Pull the right rein tighter!" " No, no, no; the right—the left!" " Keep your seat for God's sake—don't move!"

Hilda felt an involuntary shudder, and an irrepressible desire to go and see what was the matter. Her book dropped on the seat, and she ran, rather than walked, to the railings, where every one else in the garden also had collected. She saw at first nothing but a great crowd on the opposite side of the road.

"Do you know what has happened?" she asked of a person next her, a nursery-maid, holding a little child in her arms.

" The horses ran away, Miss, and I think they got entangled in the bar opposite, for they drove right against it, and haven't moved since."

Hilda stood, her eyes fixed on the spot; she shook from head to foot. Presently, the crowd that had gathered, moved a little, and she saw a carriage, almost on its side, but so smashed, that it was impossible to recognize anything more than that it was an open barouche. The horses were down, and now both still.

Hilda could bear her anxiety no longer, she thought she saw some one being dragged out of the carriage, and she felt it was her aunt.

She unlocked the gate as quickly as she could, but her hand was trembling so, that it seemed to be ages before she could make the key turn.   She did not wait to close it, but rushed, heedless of all the horses and carriages that were about, amongst them, till she came to the spot where the accident happened.

"You must not go into that crowd, Miss Chichester."

A firm hand took hold of her, and moved her back.

"Is it my aunt? Oh, tell me, is she hurt?" and she raised her eyes, swimming with tears, to Walter Wentworth.

She did not seem surprised at seeing him, the shock she received, the horror she felt for fear her aunt should be injured—for she was certain now it was her carriage, she was near enough to see it now, smashed as it was —all took off any surprise she would otherwise have felt.

He had not answered, but he put her arm in his and led her away. She had not gone ten steps, however, before she stood quite still, and said,

" Where are you taking me to ? I must see my aunt. Why should I not go there?" and she turned as if she were going back, and at the same time, drew her arm away.

Walter saw she was intending to go, and as he knew she could only see a sight too horrible for her eyes if it could be avoided, he said, firmly, but gently,

" I shall not let you go there. I am going to take you home, and your aunt will be home immediately."

At first, her old feeling of fear came over her as he spoke, but it lasted only a moment, and his words, that her aunt would be home immediately, only made her anxiety greater ; she thought something very dreadful had happened, and that he would not let her know it till she got home.

"But you have no right to prevent me, I will go," and she again attempted to take her arm away; but he was as determined as she was, and held her fast.

"Listen, Hilda; whether I have right or not on my side, I care not; but if I offend you so as to make it impossible for you ever to forgive me, I shall still insist on making you leave this spot, and taking you home. It is for your own sake," he added, a little more gently, "but if you won't do it for yourself, do it for me."

She made no further opposition, and he led her back through the gardens as she had come, home. When they reached the door he said,

"Tell your aunt's servant she may be wanted, so to be ready, and I shall be back directly."

As soon as she had gone in, he told the servant who had opened the door that an accident had occurred to Lady Fordyce, that

they had better at once send for Brodie and
Hancock, and to be in readiness at the door
for her to be carried up to her room. As
soon as he had given these directions, he
hurried back to the scene of horror he had
saved Hilda from witnessing. It was in
truth an awful sight. Poor Lady Fordyce
was on the grass, where they had laid her
till a stretcher was brought from the St.
George's Hospital to carry her home on,
her eyes were open, but fixed; the blood
streaming down the side of her head, which
was uncovered; her arm lying on her breast
with her hands clenched; her dress all torn,
and in several places spots of blood; one
of her legs so bent up that it could not have
been in that position had it not have been
broken, and the other covered over by
her shawl, that had fallen off her. One
could not tell whether she was pale, her face
was so smeared with blood, but the con-

tracted lips showed the agony she was suffering.

Walter got up to her just as the stretcher
arrived, he helped to lift her on, and the only
signs of life she gave were deep groans as
they moved her. He directed all, and he
was prompt and decisive in all he did; the
servants looked to him, they knew him to
be a friend of the family, and were glad to
have any one they could look to for some
direction.

The footman, who had been thrown off
the box, but with no injury save a few
bruises, came up to him and said,

"The poor coachman, Sir, I fear, is done
for; what is the best thing to do about
him ?"

"Let him be carried to the hospital
directly."

"And the horse, Sir, must be shot, the
other is dead."

"Very well, go yourself to Tattersall's,

and ask some to come and do it, say it is for Sir William Fordyce."

Walter now hastened to join the men that were slowly carrying poor Lady Fordyce home; he remembered he had left the gates of the gardens open after taking Hilda back, and he now made them go that way, as it saved some yards by not going round by the gate. And then he went forward to have the door of the house open; but that was needless, all in the house knew of the accident, and were ready to do all that human beings could. Sir William was not at home, it was fortunate; men on such occaions are best away, if they are much interested, for they cannot control themselves, and they are of no use.

"Carry her at once to her own room," was Walter's direction to the men as they moved on, bearing her as gently as they could up the stairs. As they reached the landing by the drawing-room door they

paused a moment to rest, Hilda was waiting
on the next by her aunt's bed-room door.
Hearing a number of steps she looked over,
and seeing them carrying her up, she feared
she was dead; she gave a slight scream, and
covered her eyes over. Walter heard and
saw her, he passed by the people and ran
up to her; his heart was so filled with pity
that he cared not what he said or did to
comfort, provided he succeeded. He led her
to her aunt's room.

"This is a sad blow to you, but you must
bear up."

"She's not dead?"

"No, no, and we must trust in God
that it is not so bad as it seems; but, dearest
Hilda, they are coming up, don't you think
you had better go away till she is laid on
her bed, and some of the marks of her
accident removed from her?"

"Oh no, let me stay, I will be very quiet,

but don't make me go, she will like to have me with her."

So she stayed, and they were now at the door; they brought her in and left her on the stretcher till the surgeons should come, thinking that moving her again would only be additional torture. Hilda went up and knelt down beside her, but she did not look, she covered her face over—she feared doing so —she heard the murmured groans, and knew that she still lived; but she had never seen any accident, and she shrank from it as nature shrinks from all that has to do with death.

"I can do no good here now," said Walter, "I will wait in the drawing-room till the doctor comes, and then I must see after the coachman, but I will be back as soon as possible."

In the midst of the sorrow the poor girl was in, it was a comfort to know he was near, and would be near to soothe and help her.

Hancock and Brodie soon arrived, when Walter told them as quickly as possible what had happened, and they ran up the stairs two steps at a time, they felt no time was to be lost. They walked in straight to the room, they could not well make a mistake, for those servants that dared not go in, were weeping outside, for all loved Lady Fordyce. She was a kind, gentle mistress, and she happened to have, what few are fortunate enough to meet with, servants who could appreciate her.

There were several in the room; Mr. Hancock said, as soon as he was in, "Let two servants remain, the rest can leave the room; and you, my dear," addressing Hilda, "let me come where you are, if you have strong nerves you may stay and help me, if not, go down till I send for you."

Hilda raised her pale face, so ashy pale that Mr. Hancock no longer left her the option of remaining.

"There, go down stairs, my dear, at once, and don't attempt to come into this room till I let you."

She went out directly, without uttering a word of opposition, and walked down stairs. She sat down on a chair close to the open door, so that no one could go up or down without her seeing them. How earnestly she prayed her aunt might be spared to her, her whole being seemed immersed in that one prayer. Every minute seemed an hour to her, for the doctor's voice had roused her to something like consciousness; though she had moved and gone about, she could tell nothing of what had passed or what she had done, from the time she ran out of the Apsley Gardens till Hancock had sent her down stairs. She had an indistinct notion of Walter being mixed up with it all, but she was only alive to the circumstances as they occurred at the moment, to look back on them was impossible.

She had not been long watching, though it seemed hours to her, before she heard a double knock at the street door. She thought it was her uncle, but she did not hope it, for how awful would be the news to him.

She jumped up, and stood at the top of the stairs. At the same time, she saw Walter come in. It was a relief, for she trusted that when her uncle did come home, there would be something to tell him that would soften the sorrow in store for him.

Walter came up, and asked her why she was there, and alone. She told him she had been sent out of the room. He led her into the back drawing-room, he so feared she might hear some sound from her aunt's room that would but add to her distress, and could do no good.

" Mr. Hancock is clever, is he not ?" asked Hilda.

" As clever, if not more so, than any man

in London. He is the head surgeon of Charing Cross Hospital, and I am certain, whatever can be accomplished by human aid, he can do, and he has Brodie with him."

" I wish my uncle was at home, and yet, when I heard you knock, and thought it was him, I was glad it was not, for it would be better the doctor should have done whatever they find necessary before he comes. Don't you think I might go up, I feel as if I could bear to see her now."

" I thought Mr. Hancock told you not to go till he sent for you."

" Yes, he did, but I think he was afraid I should do more harm than good."

" Never mind what you think ; if he told you not to go, depend upon it, he meant it, and you must stay here."

" Can't you go and see how she is ? It seems such a long time since I came down."

" I will go, but you must remain here till I come back."

He went, and came back in a few minutes;
he was afraid she might follow him if he did
not return, and he could not bear the thought
of her suffering needlessly, which she must
have done had she gone up then, for poor
Lady Fordyce was having her leg set. It
was broken three inches above the knee.
Hancock was afraid of giving her chloroform,
in the state she was in, and the pain she endured must have been very great.

Wentworth went in; he asked no questions, it was not necessary, he saw what was
being done, and then he returned to Hilda.

"Did you see her?" she asked, before he
was quite down the stairs.

"Yes, I went in; but Hancock was setting her leg, and so I did not speak. I
know it does not do to interrupt with questions at such a moment."

"Is her leg broken, then?" and Hilda
covered her face with her hands, as if she
feared seeing it.

" Yes," replied Wentworth, " but a broken
leg, well set, is not the worst accident that
can befall a person."

Hilda made no answer, she sat there im-
moveable; but he saw how she suffered then.
Not a tear dimmed her eye, and he longed to
say something to soothe her. It was indeed
a trying moment, even to him.

" I will wait with you till they come
down, as, perhaps, there may be something
wanting that I can do."

" Oh, don't go ll my uncle comes home,
I could not stay alone."

" I will stay, if it will be any comfort to
you. You don't know what I would give to
be able to say anything, or do anything that
would lighten your sorrow."

He took her into the room, and sat down
on a sofa beside her. They were still able
to see the stairs, in case any one came, or
wanted them.

" Would you like me to fetch Sir William? I daresay I should find him at his club."

"No, don't leave me," was all she said, and she shrunk up closer to him. He put his arm round her, and gently laid her head down on his shoulder.

"My poor Hilda, how I wish I could guard you from every sorrow through life. This is the first trouble that has ever befallen you, and so it seems more hard to bear, but you must not yet look to the darkest side; we can hope, and I do hope, and you must try to do so, too."

"But supposing Mr. Hancock says there is none? What shall I do? My dear, dear auntie! You don't know how good she is! And if she were to die, I should lose the only being who really loves me in the world!"

"You must not talk so, Hilda, you have many who love you; and listen, darling, though it is not a time to be talking or thinking of oneself, you must never say that to me again. You know what I mean, do you not?" and he pressed her in his arms, and kissed her pale forehead. "Tell me, Hilda, that you understand me and believe me, and that you will always trust me, whatever happens."

"I do believe you, and trust you; and even in my greatest sorrow, I feel it makes me so happy to hear you say so, for I sometimes fancied you did not love me, and then I cannot tell you how miserable I was."

"Then, my own treasure, you must never let such foolish fancies enter your head again," and he stroked her soft, wavy hair.

Hilda could not have believed that joy and sorrow could be felt so intense at the same moment—and yet so it was. She knew he loved her, which was unspeakable joy to her, and she believed her aunt, who, next to Wentworth, was the dearest being on earth to her, was dying, which she felt was, indeed, a bitter, acute grief.

They had remained as they were for some minutes without speaking, when Wentworth gently drew his arm away, and raising her head, got up. He had heard a movement up-stairs, and a door open.

"Where are you going?" she asked.

"You stop here a minute, dear Hilda, and I will come back to you. I think the doctors are coming down."

"Let me hear what they say, will you?"

"Yes, I will bring them in to you."

She waited patiently till he came back with Mr. Hancock; Brodie had left.

It was a strange thing the influence Wentworth had over her, she was like an obedient child in his hands, she, who had always been so spoilt, and accustomed to have her own way; but she had found it impossible to resist him, the only time she had ever attempted it, she had failed, and she no longer had any desire to do so. She fancied *now* he had a right to her submission, and she felt a pleasure at being thwarted, for the new sensation it gave her of being obliged to give in.

"I am afraid, my dear young lady, I cannot say much to relieve your anxiety. I have explained to Mr. Wentworth how your aunt is, and I will leave him to tell you— he will do so better than I can; and I must hasten away, as I have much to do, and it will be necessary for me to be here again in an hour or two," and so Mr. Hancock hurried out, either because he was really pressed for time, or that Hilda's pale, sorrowful, and beautiful face made him fear any questions he would rather not answer.

She watched him till he was so far down the stairs that she could no longer see him, and then she slowly turned her eyes to Wentworth; but his face looked so stern and grave, she knew he had determined to go

through a painful task and not shrink from
it. They stood for a second; she fearing to
ask, he fearing to tell. But it was but for a
moment he gave way. IIe had a strong,
firm will, and he rarely allowed any heart's
feelings to interfere with it, but there had
been a moment's struggle this time.

"Come with me for five minutes in the
boudoir." He took her in and made her sit
down; he himself paced up and down the
little room. He was wondering why Fate
had decreed he should be the means of telling her this sad news. Why should he have
been involuntarily thrown across her again,
when he had determined to avoid her at all
times and in all places; and her openly
confessing her love for him, only placed him
in a more painful position. It was true he
had drawn it from her, but that did not alter
the fact. However, whatever happened now,
he would keep to his word, she would trust

him, and he would not prove unworthy of the trust.

Hilda sat for some time watching him, with his head bent down and his eyes on the ground, but she could not bear the suspense any longer. She had twice asked him to tell her, but her voice had been low and his thoughts had so occupied him that he had not heard her; so she got up, and putting her hand on his arm to arrest him, said in a calm tone that however cost her much to assume, but she did it for his sake.

"I am ready to listen to what you have to tell me, and I am prepared for the worst." The last words were uttered in rather a faltering voice, but her face remained the same. He put his arms round her and pressed her to his heart.

"Don't look so, Hilda. I would rather see you agitated than this unnatural calmness. It is, indeed, necessary for you to be

prepared for the worst, for it is God's will
that the worst should happen—"

He heard one choking, suffocating sob,
but nothing more; a moment after she lifted
up her pale face to his, and there was a child-
like confidence in her expression as she
said—

"How long can she live? I know you
will tell me the truth?"

"It may be weeks," he replied, "but it
may not be more than days. Mr. Hancock
will be better able to judge when he comes
this evening."

"My poor aunt!" was all she said, but in
a voice that made Wentworth's heart ache.

Presently she asked what were the injuries
she had sustained, and where? He told her
the fatal injury was in the head, but that her
leg was broken in two places; she was not
conscious, but the moment she was, Hilda
was to be called.

" But may I not go at once to her ?" she asked.

" I think you had better not; you had better wait till you are sent for. Hancock said it would be better for both of you."

There was a loud peal at the house bell and a knock, quick and short, that Hilda knew well to be her uncle's.

" Oh, you go down to him—don't let the servants tell him—you break it to him—make haste, make haste, before they open the door !" And Walter went to soften to Sir William the blow that was so soon to descend upon him.

CHAPTER II.

SIR WILLIAM FORDYCE, as we have seen, was not a man of very sensitive or acute feelings, but yet the horrible news that greeted him on his return home was a heavy sorrow to him, for he loved his wife as dearly as he could love anything. Walter told it him as gently as he could; he spared him, as much as possible, the dreadful details, for he knew he would learn them soon enough. He said he would go up at once to her; and though Wentworth assured him it would be no comfort to her, as she was still unconscious, and only harrow his own feelings, he persisted, and he went up, Wentworth with him.

As they passed the drawing-room, Wentworth stopped Sir William and brought him in to poor Hilda, who at that moment was grieving more for him than for herself. He kissed her gently on her forehead. Their grief, for the same cause, drew them together. She saw he was going up.

"Oh, let me go with you, it is dreadful staying here!"

He told her to come, and turning round to Wentworth, asked if he could remain, it would be a comfort to him if he was near. Wentworth felt he might be useful; and his heart, cold and selfish as it was at times, yet was deeply grieved for the affliction of Sir William and Hilda. He said he would return in an hour.

Sir William and his niece entered the room, where poor Lady Fordyce lay groaning piteously, but yet unconscious to everything but the pain she was suffering. It was a fearful sight to see the mutilated body lying there, writhing with agony, that a few hours before had been full of life and health. There was no fear of disturbing her; there was no need for all the caution they took to be quiet. She heard nothing.

Men have seldom the courage in a sick-room that a woman has. Sir William, on entering the room with noiseless steps, put his hand over his eyes; he was afraid to face what might meet his gaze. He stood at the door. Hilda took his hand and gently led him up to the side of the bed his poor wife was lying on. He then removed his hand, he was ashamed of his own weakness; but when he saw the distorted countenance, the head, with the blood still flowing, though but slightly, through the bandages, he could not bear it. He groaned, too, but his was mental suffering, and the tears rolled down his cheek, the first he had shed since his childhood.

It was now Hilda's turn to comfort. And yet she knew not what to say; her own heart was ready to burst at the awful, ghastly sight before her, but she had strength not to give way; and yet she had dreaded seeing her aunt more than Sir William had done, for she had submitted to the reasons for not going to her sooner, whereas her uncle had not; he had insisted on going, and now sank beneath the blow.

"It is very, very awful, dear uncle, but you must not give way; you must bear up, for it is God who has sent us this affliction, and, therefore, it must be for our good; and if you grieve so now you will wear all your strength away, and not be able to be here when she may most need you."

Her words did good, for it caused his tears to flow more freely, and gradually he became quieter. He knelt down by the side of the bed, and took one of his poor wife's hot hands in his; it was so closely clenched that it was with difficulty he opened it, and the print of her nails was so deep, that it had nearly broken the skin. As he knelt there he prayed. He prayed that God would spare her more agony, if not her life. It was long, long since he had prayed so from his heart. He now rose from his knees, and Hilda gave him a chair. He sat down, still holding her hands. Her cries of pain were not so loud nor so frequent, and by degrees they ceased; and she seemed to have fallen into a kind of sleep, but it was not a sleep that would do her much good, she still was too restless.

Hilda was standing by Sir William watching her aunt. They had been so some time, neither knew how long; but they were afraid even of exchanging signs for fear of disturbing her. Presently the handle of the door turned in that cautious way that people always use if they fear disturbing any one, and Mr. Hancock came in. He signed to Sir William not to move, and he walked up slowly and gently till he was beside them; he then looked at the poor suffering woman, and then beckoned to him to follow him out of the room. But in disengaging his hand from her's, Sir William roused her, for she had grasped him so tightly, a faint scream followed, and the groans of pain began again.

Mr. Hancock, as she had been disturbed, profited by the opportunity, and redid the ligatures about the head that had become slightly displaced, and then he left the room with Sir William, whispering to Hilda to remain; she was glad, however, when they returned, for there was a nervous fear upon her, when left alone so, with one so near death. Mr. Hancock merely looked at her, gave his directions to the servants, and left.

Though Sir William had with his own

eyes seen the state his wife was in, still the shock seemed as great as if nothing had happened, when Mr. Hancock told him he thought it his duty to let him know at once what he thought of the case, that a few days would terminate all her sufferings. When he returned to her bedside, he seemed a changed man; he looked years older; his face was haggard and drawn. He turned round to Hilda and asked suddenly—

"Is Wentworth come back?"

"I don't know," she replied, "for I have not been out of the room."

He moved towards the door, as if he was going out himself, but changed his mind, and said—

"Go down, dear, and see, and come and tell me directly he is there."

She did as she was desired. He was not come; but she had not long to wait before she saw him drive up to the door in a cab. She went to the dining-room door to meet

him, and tell him her uncle was anxious to
see him.

"How is she now?" he inquired.

"Just as when you left.   Mr. Hancock
has been; he spoke to my uncle, but I don't
know what he said, for as soon as he was
gone my uncle sent me down to wait for
you."

"It makes me so happy to think I can be
of any service to you in such a sad moment.
How pale and worn you look, Hilda; you
want rest, I am sure."

"No, indeed, I do not.   I will go now and
tell my uncle you are here."

She went up-stairs, and in a few minutes
Sir William came in.   Wentworth saw the
change a few hours had wrought in him; it
was, indeed, visible enough.

"Wentworth, I cannot tell you how much
I feel all your kindness," he said, shaking
hands warmly with him, "and I want to
take advantage of it, for this dreadful shock

has rendered me perfectly unfit for every-thing," and he drew his hand across his brow, as if to clear his thoughts, for he paused.

"I assure you, Sir William, I hope you will make use of me in any way you like, for I returned here merely to see if I could be of any service," said Walter.

"Are you aware of the hopeless state of my poor wife?" asked Sir William.

"Mr. Hancock told me when he left the first time," replied Wentworth; "but I yet trust it may not be so bad as he fears. You must not despond. It must be very dread-ful to see her suffer so, but that he told me would not continue."

"No," replied Sir William, "because when once mortification takes place, pain ceases; but I would not wish her live as she is, for where she to do so, she would always suffer. Poor Mary! poor Mary!"

He walked up and down the room, his

hands behind him, and his head hanging down; but in a few minutes he seemed to remember that he was going to make a request of Wentworth, and that he had not yet done so; he stopped suddenly, and said—

"You know Mrs. Phillips, don't you? Well, being Lady Fordyce's daughter, it is but right I should send and let her know; but then—" and Sir William hesitated.

"You are afraid of any sudden excitement, such as Mrs. Phillips coming, might be injurious to Lady Fordyce."

"Exactly, that is exactly what I wanted to say; and I think it would be much better if she could be persuaded not to come until to-morrow at all events," said Sir William, quite relieved; for he did not like to tell the truth, that in his present state he could not bear to see or hear her, and of course she would remain if she came.

Walter undertook the mission, though it

was not one he would have chosen. Before he left, Sir William pressed him very much to come back—it was friendly, so kind of him to have exerted himself so much for them in their sorrow.

Poor Sir William! he seemed suddenly to have quite changed his opinion of Walter Wentworth, for he had never professed to like him; there was a stern, cold manner in him that always made him feel uncomfortable, and he was uneasy till he was out of reach of its influence. But now he was glad to have him there, near him, and to feel he would be at hand in case of need.

His having been an eye-witness of the sad calamity that had fallen on them, he having been so active and prompt in all he did afterwards, and then the kind manner in which he had told him the mournful tale, had all conduced to make him not only feel friendly, but grateful towards him. He wondered how he ever could have disliked a man who could have shown so much sympathy for him when in such deep grief.

As he walked up-stairs to his wife's room, he determined to make amends in the future for any want of cordiality there had hitherto been in his manner towards him.

Sir William could not be considered a bright specimen of the human race, yet there were many upright points in his character. He only required being led right, and he continued so till some evil spirit came and nudged him, and whispered something about being weak, and silly, and led away by any foolish person that chose, and then he soon lost his way, and had not the good spirit appeared soon, he might have gone on to ruin.

A week had elapsed since the accident had taken place. It had been spent by Sir William and Hilda in alternate hopes and fears, though hope, from the commencement, had been quite excluded from them. Still, one will hope, even against reason. Hope is a living spirit within us, it suffers when we do, it rejoices when we are happy. It is sometimes strong, sometimes weak, but never dies till death severs us; and then, and then only, does hope die, too. It sometimes reasons against itself, but then it is too strong to be conquered, and can venture to be its own antagonist.

Walter Wentworth was constantly there, but it seemed as if he knew exactly when he was wanted, for he was never to be seen but when there was something he could do.

Sir William's first question in the morning was, " Is Mr. Wentworth here ?" His last request at night, if he happened to be there, was, " Pray come to-morrow."

But Walter understood too well what was best; he always avoided coming if he knew the Chichesters, Phillips's, or Grahams were there, and it required Hilda's help for him to steer well clear of them, for they all of them were there, especially the Phillips's, as often as possible. Indeed, Sir William had positively to refuse Mrs. Phillips coming to stay altogether, till, as she said, her mother was better, and she even appealed to her mother, to make her say she wished her to do so; but Sir William could be obstinate, and he was on this occasion. He told her that it would entail more trouble, having another person living in the house, she could call and see her mother whenever she wished, but he could not have anything more.

Captain Phillips recommended her not going too far about it, because it might lead to a quarrel, and then, when her mother died, of course, Burwood would be closed to them. So Mrs. Phillips wisely took her husband's advice, and gave up insisting on taking up her entire abode in Park Lane.

It would have been a sad torment to them all if she had, and most especially, to the poor dying woman herself, for she shrunk more than ever from her daughter's disagreeable voice and hard manners.

When Mrs. Phillips first came, she shrieked, and kicked, and was carried out of her mother's room by dint of sheer force, in violent, but probably assumed, hysterics. The poor invalid felt shocked at seeing her daughter so affected, for she believed it to be caused by real grief.

However, when Mr. Hancock came, and found his patient more excited, and more feverish than usual, he desired, on hearing the cause, that no one should be admitted inside the room, who was unable to control themselves a little more than Mrs. Phillips seemed able to do.

It had its effect. The next time she went she was quite calm, and forgot that it was right and fashionable in a lady to be overcome on such occasions.

Next to her husband and niece, none

grieved more at the prospect of losing her friend and sister-in-law than Mrs. Chichester. She owed her so much for all her thought and care of her child, for all her many little kindnesses to herself, that she had learnt to love her very dearly. She regretted now that on the very day the accident occurred, indeed, within an hour—for it was in going home from the Grahams, after having been to Edward Square—that she had spoken about Hilda and Mr. Wentworth in a way she feared Lady Fordyce thought unnecessary. She determined, if possible, to say something about it, that there should not be any feeling but one of confidence and affection between them.

Lady Fordyce, at times, was tolerably free from pain, but it was only occasionally.

It was on Friday evening, nearly a fortnight after the fatal Saturday. Lady Fordyce's bed was moved, in the day-time, close up to the window, that she might have as much air as possible, for they had not been able to move her from her bed, the slightest touch causing a paroxysm of agony.

She was laying there now, her face was less painful than usual to look at. It was still drawn and frightfully pale, but the eyes seemed more natural, there was a weary, longing expression in them, as she gazed up at the blue sky, as if she wished to be up there, and at rest.

There was a gentle knock at the door, and Mrs. Chichester came in. She was a quiet, loving woman, and Lady Fordyce always welcomed her with a smile. Her voice was not loud like Mrs. Graham's, and she was not always telling her she ought to be doing precisely the opposite to what she was doing, as Mrs. Phillips invariably did. Rose's company soothed her, and besides, she was her darling Hilda's mother, and were it only on that account, she must love here.

To-day, she had been thinking much

about Hilda, and her future, when she would
be no more ; for she was quite aware that,
probably, a few weeks, at longest, would be
the span of her time here on earth.

Illness generally makes one view everything in a new light, and when it is an illness unto death, how much more so ? What
in life we could not understand, is, in death,
made plain to us. What, then, we were
blind to, now we see clearly enough. And
how changed are our earthly views as to
riches and grandeur ! In our dying hour,
we wonder why we fought, why we struggled
for that, which now we not only leave without regret, but that we long to be severed
from.

Lady Fordyce thought this, and felt it.
She longed to be released from her sufferings,
and the parting from her worldly goods
would never have crossed her mind; but
she did fear, she did dread the parting with
her heart's idol.

There is but one pang in death to the true Christian, and that is, leaving those dear to them, leaving them to battle on through life's campaign alone; *that* seems hard. We would take all those we love along with us; not from any selfish motives—that, in such a moment, would be impossible—but for their sakes, to save them all further trials, sorrows, and disappointments. But that is not permitted—and wisely so. Each must go their weary journey through life; each must pass from this world to the next, with but one companion, the companion of all who ask and seek for Him.

Lady Fordyce had been wishing, during the last three or four days, that she might be able to speak to Mrs. Chichester about Hilda, and now both the power and the opportunity were given her.

She opened the subject at once, after their mutual greeting was over.

"Rose, I have a great weight on my mind

and heart, and I wish and must talk to you
freely and openly on the subject, or else I
should not leave this world, as I hope and
trust I may do, perfectly, undisturbedly
happy. You know what the pang will be—
if there should be any—in dying. You
know Hilda has been, and is so dear to me,
that I have not dared to realize the cer-
tainty of parting with her, of leaving her,
so young and so beautiful, to the world's
temptations. I know what you would say,
dear Rose," said Lady Fordyce, on Mrs.
Chichester appearing desirous of speaking,
"you would tell me, you, as her mother,
can guard her, and keep her from harm.
But, remember, she will be away from your
influence, she will be launched forth into the
world with all the dangerous freedom of a
married woman. Hilda, too, is naturally of
an obstinate disposition, and tenacious of in-
terference; I doubt if she would submit to
anyone but her uncle when I am gone. She

is fond of him, and he has become so of her, but I think he even would find it a difficult task to succeed, were he to try her very much. She requires great gentleness; anything like harshness or severity would close up the warm springs of her heart. My poor child! my darling Hilda! oh, that I could watch over you till you need none to do so, that I could bear and suffer for you what you may have to endure! Oh, that I could remove the thorns out of your path!"

The tears slowly fell from Lady Fordyce's eyes, she felt a conviction, a presentiment, some might call it, that Hilda's path would be a thorny one; and she, poor woman, in her desire, as she said, to remove them, thought of a plan that seemed to do so at one fell swoop.

Mrs. Chichester tried to console her, and to cheer her about Hilda, but in vain; she seemed so confident that trouble was in store for her, unless her plan was carried out, that she determined at once to say what it was; and so she, who would, if she could, have shed drops of blood to save Hilda even an unhappy thought, laid the train that was to end in her entire misery.

Oh, how blind we mortals are! how we work and work, imagining we are all the time doing some great deed, some wonderful piece of diplomacy; and we open our eyes to find we have cut our own throats, that we have just accomplished, just succeeded, after anxiety, suspense, and trouble, in that which we would give the best years of our life to undo.

God is very good when he denies some of our prayers. We most of us have lived, however young we may be, long enough to know what it is to be grateful. Some wish, which, at the time, we imagined would be the completion of our happiness, has not been gratified; we even wondered we ever could have desired such a thing, it seemed so preposterous.

Have any of my readers ever kept a journal? If so, let them turn back a few months, and see what their hopes were then, and what they are now.

Mrs. Chichester scarcely knew of any cause that should make her sister-in-law so anxious about Hilda; she saw and felt that it was a sad and serious loss for her child, but she could not tell beyond that why it should be so bitter a thought to her.

"Hilda will be as much exposed to the dangers that you seem to fear for her in her married life, dear Mary, as if you are spared to her. She will, of course, be at a very great distance from all her own; but, surely, she will have a sufficient protection and a better guide in her husband than any one else could be to her. And you must not create difficulties; she has had a bright, happy youth, and she owes it all to you."

" Stop, Rose, you don't know what I have
done. Now that it is too late, my eyes are opened to the injudicious way I have acted with
regard to her. I thought I watched so carefully, I thought I would shield her by my
great care from all the sorrows we are born
to in this world. I want to tell you, Rose,
what, in my folly, I would not even admit to
myself, still less to you, on that day—that day
which was almost my last of life. When
you spoke to me of Mr. Wentworth being
too much with us, and that people would
make remarks, and what is worse, and the
only thing I could care for, Hilda might
learn to prefer him to others, I would
scarcely listen to you, and I felt vexed you
should say so; and yet, Rose, I had just
then been talking to Hilda, and she had told
me she did not wish to become David Graham's wife, and it was only on her seeing my
tears, that she at last promised to fulfil all
my wishes on that subject. Then, and even

when you spoke to me, I would not believe
she cared for Walter Wentworth, and I do
not believe so now; I think, perhaps, she
ceases to like, for she never did love, David,
from that cause. But I now see how wrong
I was to have allowed him to continue igno-
rant of her engagement; but I never saw
anything in his manner but what was perfectly cold and distant."

Lady Fordyce waited a few minutes, the
talking tired her; but she was so anxious to
say all before the pain should return, she
feared not having another opportunity.

"I told Mr. Wentworth of Hilda being
engaged to Mr. Graham the night of your
ball, and his only answer was that he had
heard so," said Rose.

"Thank God, then, for it will render it
much more easy for me to accomplish the
only wish I have, connected with this
world."

"What is that?" asked Mrs. Chichester.

" It is that I may see Hilda, David's wife before I die."

Mrs. Chichester started, and Lady Fordyce turned her head round as much as it was in her power to move it, to see her sister-in-law's face.

" Why are you astonished, Rose? Is it not a very natural desire? and the only one, I am certain, that will ensure Hilda's happiness. I shall die without a regret, without a wish, and perfectly happy, if I see that first."

" But—" said Mrs. Chichester, hesitating.

" You would say, if I wish to see it whilst I am living, it must be at once, immediately. Well, yes, why not? I know, perhaps, every day may be my last, and you know now why I am so anxious."

" Who do you propose to speak to first about it?"

" I shall tell Mrs. Graham, and when once

she has arranged with David, 1 will speak to Hilda about it. You don't think, Rose, she cares even the very least for Mr. Wentworth? That would, indeed, be awful! I would rather sacrifice my own wishes a million times over, if I dreamt for one second she had even a preference for him."

"No, truly and sincerely I do not, nor do I think he cares for her; it is only Arthur has that idea in his head, and I thought it all imagination at the time. It was he made me tell him of her engagement, and also speak to you. I did both, as you know, but it was with a firm conviction that there was not the slightest necessity for either."

"Though I felt the same conviction myself, it is unspeakable comfort to hear you say so. I shall tell Mr. Hancock to-day what I wish, and make him tell me how short, or how long he thinks my stay amongst you will be permitted, though when once that is over, and I leave my darling, I

trust safe and happy, I care not how soon
I am released, for I can then do no more
for her, I can only pray God to watch over
her and shield her from evil."

CHAPTER III.

WHY is it mothers are more blind to
the welfare of their children than the most
indifferent of their acquaintances? Why is
it if a child is consumptive, or otherwise,
those who care not whether it lives or dies,
see it, and pity the poor mother who is so
soon to be deprived of what she holds so
dear? She hears remarks about her child,
looking thinner and paler, or that it is weak,
or has a cough, and a mild climate is recommended. All the hints are useless, they fall
on her ears like a remark on the weather
might do.

And yet it is not that the mother is a

careless or unfeeling parent, far from it, she idolizes her child, but she wilfully deceives herself, she won't see it because the thought is painful to her. Truth always is. So a mother is the last to see if her child is risking her whole heart's happiness, she will throw her in the way of those she knows it would be ruin to regard in any other light than of a mere friend, the more fascinating they are of course the more they are welcomed, it renders it agreeable to her other friends, and the mother thinks her child's safe-guard is the utter impossibility of any other feeling being consonant with common sense, that is, the common sense that belongs to the wealth-seekers of this world.

A mother could not imagine her child guilty of such utter folly as falling in love with a man who is too poor to marry, or with a man who, though good enough to come and eat her dinners and amuse her guests after dinner with all the last new songs, is far from being a fit match for her daughter. No; it is very pleasant to know such people, for they are convenient. Though it is these kind of men that young ladies think much more suited to them and their tastes than those honest, bluff, fat, red-headed men, with their pockets well filled, and broad acres of flourishing well-paying lands. And yet, not any little fool going but that will see and notice the flirtation, the soft looks, the manœuvre to sit by each other at dinner, or to go down to supper together, or to get a quiet game at chess —for chess must be quiet, and so suits their purposes. All these, and a thousand other little cleverly managed excuses for being thrown together is visible enough to the passing stranger, but wholly unperceived by the anxious parent, who is ever on the watch to guard her child against such evils. But she wilfully shuts her eyes, she won't

allow herself to believe anything so unpleasant.

Man, when in love, is totally blind to
his mistress' defects. She may be ugly to
the world, but she is beautiful to his eyes;
she may be stout, and he may have a very
peculiar objection to a stout person; but
though it is possible he thought her actually
fat on their first introduction, his eyes,
from the transformation love accomplishes
on those orbs, will gradually lessen her, till
he actually thinks her slight and delicate-
looking. He deliberately sets to work to
persuade himself that truth is false.

The human life is false and deceitful by
origin. Nothing we say, and very little we
do, is strenuously honest and truthful. There
is an indescribable attraction in falsehood,
that most find so hard to resist, they let
the spell act. It is not even each other
we deceive, we deceive ourselves, and unfortunately very frequently succeed. False-

hood is so easy, comes so naturally, always
seems the most agreeable, always appears
to please every one. It seems so hard that
one cannot gratify oneself and our friends
when it is so easily done. And so we lie
on, and think we sin not. It is not those
who unconsciously try to screen truth from
themselves or others that are wandering from
that straight and narrow path so few can
find, but it is those who deliberately, knowing
realities, substitute fictions.

And so poor Lady Fordyce is not amongst
the latter, but amongst the former. She in
her heart believed that Hilda's affections were
still free; but Mrs. Chichester had every now
and then a voice whispering within her, that
told her Hilda's feelings were not so entirely
under her own control as she told Lady
Fordyce she believed, but she deceived her
from a charitable motive, she thought it
would save her such pain and anxiety, she

did not consider she was sacrificing her own child.

When she went down stairs after leaving Lady Fordyce she, as usual, went in to see Hilda, and tell her that she might go up to her aunt; she found Walter Wentworth there with her daughter. He was just leaving, Hilda had told him her mother would probably soon be down, and therefore, if he did not wish to see her he had better leave and return, for Sir William could not bear Wentworth to be away when he was at home.

Truth, my dear reader, is ill-bred. You do, not think any one could be so vulgar as to speak the truth? Why, don't you think it necessary to shake hands with a person who pays you a visit, and tell them you are glad to see them, when you are much more inlined to kick them out of your house. Don't you kiss a baby, and say you like kissing babies because its mother is present, when you would as soon kiss a hot piece of boiled beef fat; all these, and a thousand other instances of daily falsehood we could give, were it necessary.

But you, reader, know them as well as we do; we are, doubtless, very polite, and may proceed from a desire to please, but it is lying. It seems a hard term, but it is a true one, and so you cannot expect it to be agreeable or elegant.

A great divine, I think Dr. Paley—if wrong, I humbly beg his memory's pardon —says, "never tell an unnecessary lie."

I should like to know who ever yet could discover where the line was to be drawn; or who ever told a lie at all but thought it necessary, if even it were only for manner's sake. Deceit and falsehood are twin brothers; and it is because there is so much of both in this world, that there is such unending misery. Were the breasts of all mankind to be laid bare, and each to read the other, how different we should all be.

At first, the remedy might be worse than the disease; we should see so much to grieve us; we should find those we trusted could be trusted no more; those we loved, were not worthy of our affection; but then, when we did place our faith and heart in the keeping of another, we should see the pure casket they were to enshrine, and there would be no more doubts, no more anxious fears; it would be a holy trust we had, for it would be a true one.

Mrs. Chichester felt on seeing Hilda and Walter together, she had wilfully deceived Lady Fordyce, but then the motive was good, and she thought for once she might do evil for good to come of it. Does good ever ensue from evil? Never. It may have the appearance of doing so at the moment, but wait and see the end. When too late, regret and remorse comes, and then sorrow and repentance follow. You cannot unsay the words you have uttered, you cannot undo

the deeds you have committed; you must
abide by the result, and learn that no good
ensues from an evil thought, word, or
deed.

Lady Fordyce may, from her dying state,
have been unconscious she was trying to
shut the truth out, and trying to make her
sister-in-law do the same. She was not
satisfied with the conviction which she had
that Hilda did not love Walter, but she
wished to believe that she did not care at all
about him, in order that she might carry out
her own plan of an immediate marriage with
David, without any qualms of conscience,
which, on the other hand, she must have
had.

She knew David to be rich, and she thought
once his wife, Hilda would be happy, because
she would have no thought or dread about
her future. She forgot Hilda knew nothing
of the want of wealth, she had always had
every wish gratified, and therefore it was not

likely she would barter her heart against money, it had no attraction for her, for she knew not its value. We must lose a thing before we can judge of what it is worth to us. But had Hilda been suddenly awakened to poverty and felt its misery, she would have chosen to be the poor wife of Walter Wentworth, rather than the rich wife of David Graham.

"Are you going, mamma?" Hilda asked as her mother came in. "Is not Arthur coming for you?"

"No, dear, he could not come to-day, and I promised to be home by dinner-time, so I must be going. How very warm it is, I think I shall have to drive back."

"Oh, I will order the carriage round if you like, it will be much better than walking all that way through this hot sun."

She rang the bell and gave the order.

"It would do you good, Miss Chichester, to take a drive; you look so tired and pale,

I am sure you want a little fresh air," said Walter to Hilda.

" Oh I must go up-stairs now, I should not like to go out unless my uucle was at home, or some one sitting with my aunt. Don't you think she seems better to-day, mamma? there is such a calm look on her face."

" I fear, dear Hilda, it is but the brightening up of the flame before it quite goes out. She may linger on a few days, but I doubt if she will be spared much longer. She seems perfectly conscious of it herself, and even anxious to be freed from her sufferings."

The tears ran down Hilda's face, she could never bring herself to think calmly of her aunt's death. It was too great a loss for her to realize it, and she tried, like all of us, to comfort herself with hope; and so to feel the shock the more acutely when it did come.

" Have you heard from Mary Fenton since you wrote to her to put her off; though I suppose the two letters reached her together?" asked her mother, to turn the conversation.

"Yes, and her mother and father are obliged to come to town for a week on business, and she is coming with them, so I suppose I shall see her. I am glad of it, for she will not be so disappointed at not coming to us."

"Is that the Miss Fenton I met at Burwood about eighteen months ago?" asked Walter, "an interesting silly sort of girl."

"Well, you are not complimentary to her nor grateful," said Hilda smiling; "it is the same; but she is thought so gentle and nice, though not very pretty; and she thought you—" Hilda stopped, for she saw a stern look, that she was always afraid of, coming over Walter's handsome face. He did not ask her to go on, nor did he make any answer.

"I hope I shall see her too, when she comes, for I think her a very charming girl,"

said Mrs. Chichester, thinking it necessary
to say something, as the silence was awk-
ward.

" No fear of that, mamma," said Hilda,
" you will see her, she is sure to find you
out, and some one else, too, if I mistake
not."

The carriage was ready, so Mrs. Chichester wished her daughter good-bye, but leaving Walter still there. He thought as he
had met her, he might as well sit through
her visit, and have a few more minutes with
Hilda. There had never been a word about
marriage mooted between them, but yet they
both seemed perfectly to understand each
other. She had learnt to call him Walter,
though at first she could not do so, but he
insisted and she obeyed, he had called her
Hilda without the same difficulty, and the
name never sounded to her so pretty as when
he addressed her by it. Walter had in-
stilled into her that she must be very careful

how she allowed her family to know of their attachment, for he told her he knew that none of them liked him, excepting Sir William, and that had only been since Lady Fordyce's accident, and therefore they would naturally throw every impediment in the way to their meeting, and probably forbid his visiting the house.

It was enough for Hilda he wished it, she did not care to know his motives, and she therefore in every way tried to hide anything she thought might be regarded in the light of a preference for him. Her's was indeed a blind love, she had given up to this man her whole heart and soul, she had not a thought, a hope, a wish, but what he was the object. She loved him with all the depth and force of a first love; there was no care, no anxiety for the future, it was a bright unclouded prospect, and what could she desire now for the present than his love, and that she believed she possessed. It was truly beautiful her love, not a touch of selfishness, nor interestedness mixed with it, it was pure, holy, and innocent. And what was Walter feeling for her, what did he give her in return for all this strong, undying affection.

When he first perceived it taking root, he was flattered as most men are, and he encouraged it, as far as he dared without letting the world perceive he did so. No one ever saw Walter singling Hilda out for attentions, but he paid them in that quiet, even, cold way, that disguised what he was doing to the world, rendered them doubly pleasing to her who appreciated the delicacy that prevented her being singled out, and then talked about, as young ladies sometimes are.

He gradually became accustomed to seeing her smile of welcome, and to like it, he looked for it, and felt disappointed if he did not see it. Trifling circumstances once occurred which broke the ice, and he spoke to her of her love, and made her admit it, with the simplicity almost of a child, but he never owned any love for her, though he implied it, and she thought that was sufficient. And now the fatal accident that he had been a witness of, and had been enabled to give so much assistance at, and the sudden friendship Sir William professed for him, had tended to increase his intimacy with Hilda so much; and her clinging to him, her appealing to him on all and every occasion, for what she ought to do, had at last touched his heart, and though his love for her, if ever it could be called so at all, was all on the surface, still it was there, and helped much to influence his manner, especially when with her alone.

There is an indescribable pleasure in being perfectly alone with those we love; we do not speak, our thoughts are all so happy and peaceful.

Walter did not give her engagement with David Graham a thought, after being told by Mrs. Chichester, though he had heard it mooted before; he went to Lady Willesden, and from her had the correct account. He knew she disliked him, and that they rarely met. He had ceased to think, as he had in the beginning, that it would be a safeguard, for he had ceased to wish it. Not that he even now thought of marrying her. It was not that he would not do so; but he did not wish it, he did not care about it. He was convinced Sir William would gladly give his consent, and would, of course, if he liked the match, portion her accordingly. Still, he felt, Walter Wentworth as a bachelor, and Walter Wentworth as a Benedict, would be two distinct people.

"I don't like leaving you, Walter, but I ought to go up to my aunt—ought I not?"

"Yes, darling; and I won't keep you more than five minutes, but you must stay with me that time, for I shall not see you again to-day."

"Not see me again to-day! Why?"

asked Hilda, her countenance falling directly. "Won't you be here this evening? My uncle will be so disappointed if you do not!"

"And will his niece be disappointed, too?" he asked, looking fondly down on her.

"You always want to make me tell you how much I miss you when you are away, and how glad I am when you are here," she replied smiling, "why are you not satisfied with knowing it is so, without always insisting on my repeating it each time?"

"Because, Hilda," he replied almost sadly, "your love is the only treasure I value in life, because it stirs up my best feelings within me; it makes me sometimes feel as I used when a boy, when my mother's gentle words and sweet smile would soothe me in my greatest grief, or calm me in my greatest anger; you have the same influence over me, I feel a different being when you are near."

"You were your mother's favourite child,

G 2

were you not?" asked Hilda, "I don't wonder at it, how she must have idolized you. But yet not as I do, Walter, for I believe my aunt loves me as dearly as any mother could love a child, much more than my own mother does, and yet her love for me is not what I feel for you," and she raised her lovely eyes, that were then so grave and thoughtful.

"My dearest one, I don't deserve your love; and yet, Hilda, I could not give it up now," he added with a sigh, "I sometimes wish I had never seen you."

"Why, Walter, don't say that, or you will make me think I am the source of some sorrow to you. Why do you say you don't deserve my love? on the contrary, it is I who do not feel good enough for you; you, who are so noble, so great, so good. Oh, Walter, I wish you could see into my heart, you then might be able to understand what it is I feel for you. Do you know," she added in a lower tone, " it sometimes frightens me, for I feel as if something must happen to one of us, that it cannot continue.".

" You are nervous, my own Hilda, from the shock you lately had, and it has made you think so, but that will soon wear off."

" It is only at times I feel that, but I used to feel it even before my poor aunt's accident."

He could say nothing really to comfort her, for he felt, too, it could not long continue as it was. It must be either one thing or the other, and the one thing, to part, and as far as lay in his power, for ever, appeared the one to be done; but he did not like the thought, so he drove it out of his mind whenever it crossed it. Why should people brood over troubles if the brooding does not alleviate them. Walter, no doubt, as far as he himself was concerned, was right; but as far as it concerned Hilda, it was selfish to the last extreme. Her misery never once struck him as being the result of their present happiness, he did not think of it at all. It was merely necessary to be cautious and guarded enough in his own manner, as to leave nothing for the world to accuse him of after.

To turn the conversation, he told Hilda he had heard from Mr. Western, who was very ill, and was at length obliged to resign his consulship, and that he would soon be in England, to remain permanently.

Hilda had but a slight recollection of her kind old friend, but she knew it would grieve her mother to hear it.

Walter now took his leave, and Hilda went up to her aunt's room. She found her dozing, she was worn out with her long exciting conversation with Mrs. Chichester. Hilda was not sorry to sit quiet and think a little, she always liked doing so whenever Walter had been talking to her as he had to-day. It made her sad when he was grave, and yet she loved him best so, it seemed more suited to him to be stern, and with her there was so much tenderness with it, that she preferred it to when he seemed gay and light hearted. His countenance wore naturally a melancholy expression, and it was more suited to his dark, handsome face, and thoughtful eyes than any other. She thought of his words, that he sometimes wished he had never met her; but she could not find one single reason for his having such a wish, but though it teased her for a few minutes, she recollected his saying he prized her love more than any other earthly blessing, and she felt happy, her whole face lighted up for a moment with unalloyed joy.

A slight movement of her aunt's, accompanied by a moan, recalled her to herself; she almost reproached herself for feeling as she did, with her more than mother by her on her death-bed. She rose and went close up to her; her eyes were open, but she did not move, but continued moaning.

"Dear aunt, can I do anything for you, or get you anything?" asked Hilda.

"Mr. Hancock has not been yet, has he?" Lady Fordyce asked in a scarcely audible tone.

"Not yet, but it is very near his usual hour."

"When he comes, dear, let me be alone with him, I wish to speak to him; and will you put a little eau-de-cologne mixed with water on my forehead, it aches so?"

As Hilda was bathing her head she said, "Do you think, Hilda, if I asked you to do something that would make me die quite, quite happy, you would do it?"

"How can you ask me such a question, dearest auntie, you know there is nothing I could do for you that I would not; and anything that could make you happy, must make me so too," replied Hilda.

Poor child, she little thought what she would be called on to do.

"Thank you, my darling, God will bless you for it."

"But what is it aunt, can I do it at once, tell me?"

"Not yet, my child, but very, very soon, I won't tell you; but to-morrow, to-morrow, Hilda, I will tell you what, if you consent, will repay me for all my love and care for you."

A vague misgiving took possession of Hilda's mind. She wondered if it could be anything about Walter; she knew her aunt did not much like him; she knew her mother and brother both disliked him; and she knew they both had lately been talking to her alone. She wondered whether it was to promise not to see him again —she couldn't promise that—it was impossible. It might be to promise not to marry him—yes, that must be it. That was what her aunt wished. And what was she to do—could she promise it? No, she could not; but then, if her aunt told her she could not die happy. Oh, it was a dreadful thought. If it proved to be that—and she could imagine nothing else —she would take courage and tell her all, how she loved him, how he loved her, and that it would break her heart to give such a promise; and if she still persisted, she would ask for a few hours delay, and she would tell Walter, and do as he advised her.

It is always a great relief in any serious difficulty to decide on a line of conduct to pursue, and to make up one's mind to abide by it, to let nothing alter one's determination. So Hilda felt it to be. She knew Walter would do what was right, and at all events she would be happy in doing what he thought so, whatever it might be. She felt relieved, but a great weight still remained.

When Mr. Hancock came, Hilda left the room, and went to her own, where she remained in anxious thought till her uncle sent for her.

"Where's Wentworth?" was his first question on her entering the library.

"He's gone, uncle, he was here in the afternoon, but he could not stay, and said something about not being able to return again to-day."

"How tiresome! I wanted to ask him to go for me to the city to-morrow. Did he say he would be here to-morrow?"

"No, he didn't say so, but I should think he would," replied Hilda.

"Well, it won't do to leave it to con-jectures, sit down and write him a note, and ask him to breakfast with us at nine."

And so Hilda had to write to him—her

first letter, and she did not the least know how ·to write it. She could not begin "Dear Mr. Wentworth," still less could she begin with "Dear Walter." So she made no beginning at all, asked him to come to breakfast, as her uncle wished to see him, and signed it Hilda.

"Let me see it, Hilda," said her uncle, as she was folding it up hurriedly.

"Shall I read it to you, uncle, it's horrid to have one's letters read," she said laughing, but feeling much more inclined to cry.

"No, child, it's much more horrid to hear a letter read, give it here. What are you doing?"

Hilda had unfolded it, and was dipping the pen in ink to write a beginning and an ending, but her uncle came up before she could do so, and took the letter out of her hand. He read it, gave it her back, and told her it did very well; he made no remark upon the peculiar way it was written.

Probably had she given it to him when he asked, he would not have noticed it, but retaining it, and then seeing she was going to add something, made him curious, and he saw in one moment how matters were, that is, he saw more than really was to be seen. For he concluded that Walter had proposed, Hilda accepted, but owing to the sorrow in the house, both had too much good feeling to allude to it.

Sir William Fordyce was as delighted as it was possible for him to be with anything under the circumstances. Had it been a month ago, he would have pitied her, inasmuch as he thought Walter a different man to what he thought him now. As Hilda's husband, he thought, he could always have him near him, why should they not live with him altogether? at least, make Burwood their home. He should be grieved to part with Hilda now, now that he was to be left alone. He formed these plans in less time than it took Hilda to seal and send off her letter in. When she had done so, he went up to her and kissed her, and said,

" My little Hilda has made me feel very happy, happier than I thought I should feel for many long days."

Hope soon revived in Hilda.

CHAPTER IV.

IT is a severe task for one human creature to tell another their time is come, that it is God's will to recall the spirit He permitted to sojourn here for a space of time, that their earthly career is at an end, that all their earthly ties must be severed, that they must leave those dear to them here below, to mourn their loss, to fight on with this world's cares—such was Mr. Hancock's task; but it was made easy to him, for he had but to specify what he thought according to the calculation human science is permitted to judge by, how many weeks or days his patient had yet before her pilgrimage

was o'er. For Lady Fordyce had not asked
whether she should recover or not, she only
asked how long a time she could feel she
had yet to do one or two things she wished
done. He told her simply and plainly that
what she wished done had better not be
delayed.

"Do you mean I cannot reckon on having
three days more? What I wish done could
scarcely be before Monday, this is Friday,
but two days, that is not long. I did not
think I was so near; but do not tell me
I may hope to see Monday dawn if you
think otherwise. Believe me, dear Mr.
Hancock," and she laid her thin hand on
his arm, "I am perfectly resigned, and it
would not shock me if you told me I was
looking at the last setting of the sun this
evening; but I have one desire that I wish
to see accomplished, and then I can die
peacefully and happy, so tell me the truth."

"You may safely leave what you wish

till Monday, unless some unforseen symptom shows itself, that I see not the slightest reason for apprehending."

As soon as Mr. Hancock had left, she sent a message requesting that Mrs. Graham and Mr. David Graham would go round to see her, as she was anxious to speak to them. They came whilst Sir William and Hilda were at dinner—as soon, indeed, as the message reached them, they left. They thought it might be Lady Fordyce was dying, so they were much relieved on hearing that she was not worse than she had been.

"I was so alarmed, my dear Sir William, that I did not wait an instant; but what can she have wished to see us for so particularly this evening, I wonder."

"The shortest way is for us to go and see," said David.

There was sense in the remark, if not politely spoken. As they were going out of the room, the servant opened the door and said,

"Her Ladyship wishes Mrs. Graham to go up alone first."

So David returned and took his chair.

"Is there any news, David, to-day?" asked Sir William, seeing a not over pleased expression on his face.

"Havn't you been to the club to-day? I don't suppose I heard more than you did."

"Yes, I went to the club, but I don't seek news as younger men generally do. Somehow it happens very often I wait for all the news to be told me in casual talk, and then I hardly do more than glance over the leading articles."

"It's to be hoped you know those who do read the papers well then," grumpily answered David.

Hilda was angry at his speaking in such a tone to her uncle, and said,

"The warm weather seems to have affected your temper, David, or perhaps—no, I know what it is, you've come out without your dinner, but that's easily remedied, we will have it back directly, and you will soon catch us up."

"Neither the heat nor the want of food have affected me," replied David, " so pray don't trouble yourself on my account."

He disliked being teased by Hilda about eating, for she had once or twice thrown out such hints, that made him guess his peculiarity of being partial to good food and plenty of it was not hidden to her. It did not tend to increase his good temper.

"This news of the death of the Archbishop of Canterbury is a glorious piece of patronage for the Ministry, but a bad thing for the country; for I suppose they will put in some canting, psalm-singing fool. They ought to give it to the Bishop of

H 2

———. He is the most able and fitted man."

"Well that's news to me," said Sir William, "was his death in the morning papers?"

"No, in the Second Edition of the Globe, only now out."

"I don't agree with you," said Sir William, "as to thinking Lord ——— will not choose a proper man. It is not like a minor appointment, he dare not give it to one who is not a good churchman and capable of performing the duties efficiently and thoroughly. The Bishop of ——— would doubtless be well enough, but there are two others with stronger claims, I think, than even him. However, it is seldom one sees the right man in the right place. By the bye, David, talking of that reminds me of old Grant, how has he got on since he has had Hartley to manage the estate?"

"At first very badly," replied David,

"because Grant would not let him manage it but as he did with all his other bailiffs, interfered, and in short, did all the evil and stopped all the good. But when Hartley told him he must leave, as it was impossible ever to get matters square as long as the same system was pursued that had brought it into such a mess, and that he was not allowed to have a voice in anything, Grant got frightened, and said he would give him his own way if he would stop. That was about six or eight months ago, so that now, I hear, they are beginning to reform things, and no doubt if he is left in power, in time, he will make the land pay well enough."

"For once then the right man is in. What did Morris say the land was worth an acre when he was valuing it?"

"Why two pound, and Grant got ten shillings, but he is a stupid old fool, and any milk-maid could bamboozle him."

"Well, he's a good old fellow, if not encumbered with too much brain," said Sir William; "don't you remember him, Hilda, he was a great admirer of your's when you were in short frocks?"

"Do you mean," asked Hilda, "a white-headed, stout old man, that asked to come to Forestfern, and always rode a grey, fat pony, very like himself?"

"That's him," said Sir William.

"I remember him perfectly, and liked him exceedingly, for he used to treat me as if I had been grown up, which I fully appreciated even then. What has he been doing?"

"Buying a small estate, about ten miles from Forestfern, called Studley Manor, they cheated him in the purchase, and he has been cheated by his steward in the management of it ever since."

"Her Ladyship would be glad if Mr. David Graham could go up-stairs now," said

John, coming in with his usual solemn face.

"How exceedingly unpleasant David can make himself," said Hilda, as her cousin left the room, "and oddly enough, it being the only thing he does excel in, I suppose, is the cause of his being so so very frequently."

Sir William smiled; he perfectly agreed with Hilda, but he possessed the blessed and virtuous power of controlling his unruly member.

We must now follow David up-stairs. He walked up slowly and heavily, as if such a massive body was too much for him to support; nor did he attempt to go less noisily as he approached the sick room; though not necessary, still most people would have thought it needful to go as gently as possible. The man opened the door, and David went in. Lady Fordyce's bed had been moved from the window back into the middle of the room. Mrs. Graham was sitting in a large easy-chair by the side of it. The windows were still open, but the blinds down, and candles were lighted. Lady Fordyce held out her hand to David as he came in, she looked very worn and tired; any one who had not seen her since her accident, could never have recognized the poor, crushed, dying woman laying there, as the same strong, stout, healthy, happy being she had been a fortnight ago. David took a chair, and after asking her how she felt, they all remained silent.

David could not help perceiving, by his mother's face, that there was something of importance to discuss, but he thought he had better wait patiently till it pleased either the one or the other to tell him; but the silence continued so long, he thought it stupid, so he turned to his mother and proposed going, for fear Lady Fordyce might be fatigued.

It had been arranged between Mrs. Graham and Lady Fordyce, when they sent for David, the latter was to communicate the substance of their conversation ; but Lady Fordyce's courage seemed to fail her, why was it? Could it be that there was a wavering in her own mind as to whether she might not be laying the foundation of lifelong misery for her darling, instead of securing her a kind and faithful friend to shield her from all trouble? Was there anything in the heavy countenance before her that she thought ill-suited her earthly idol? It may have been so, but whether it was or not, she began immediately after David proposed to go, to speak, and though she spoke all the time in a low tone, there was a peculiar distinctness in each word that struck both Mrs. Graham and her son.

" You must not go, David, as I did not send for you without an object, and I must

not be tired, as I have yet to tell you what
it is." She paused a minute, and passed
her hand over her eyes as if to recollect
what she wished to say, and then continued,
" You remember when we left Burwood
the sort of engagement that existed between
you and Hilda."

" Oh, pray don't let that annoy you half
an instant," cried David, hastily interrupting
her, "I am quite aware it was more the
wish of my father and mother than of our
own, and I can quite understand that you
wish to leave your niece free and unfettered ;
believe me, I was quite prepared for this,
and, moreover, I have scarcely given the
matter a thought either way since it was
settled."

Perhaps David thought he was smoothing
the road for Lady Fordyce, instead of making
it so rough she hardly knew how to ride
over it. He spoke too in an ungracious
tone, though he did not mean it.

"You are quite mistaken, David, you have totally miscontrued my words," she replied, still in the low clear tone she had before spoken, "I was far, very far from proposing that the engagement should be broken. I wish, on the contrary, I pray most earnestly that I may live to see you man and wife."

David started, for a moment he thought her mind must be wandering; he had been told she could not live many days, and that she was aware of the fact herself; but her face and her eyes looked too placid for him to think so beyond the second.

"Do not seem surprised, David; I am aware, perhaps, even more assuredly so than you are that my days are numbered, my time is short, and that if I wish to see my hopes fulfilled, it must be done almost immediately. Hilda is very young, my great pang at the prospect of death is leaving her unprotected; for Sir William, though very,

very fond of her would not be judicious; and, moreover, a man is not a fit protection for an unmarried girl of her age. She is very beautiful, too, and has received and will receive much adulation and admiration. I would wish to leave her so situated that she would be guarded from all this, and there is none could guard her from such temptation but a husband. She has learnt to look on you as her future husband, and—" she stopped suddenly, for Hilda's words sounded clearly in her ears as she uttered them on that memorable Sunday. But had she wished it, she thought it too late to retreat now, besides, Mrs. Graham, who mistook her pause for a sort of reluctance to ask David point-blank to marry her said,

"And David, too, dear Lady Fordyce, has considered Hilda as his affianced wife, and if they have not been so much together as people similarly situated generally are, it is from no want of affection or esteem on his side, but merely that circumstances seemed always to interfere to prevent it."

"Do you think, Lady Fordyce, that Hilda has considered herself as engaged to me since we were at Burwood, because if so, she has a strange way of behaving."

"Hilda is young, David, don't forget that now, or if she becomes yours, still less then; she has a warm, loving heart, but she requires leading, not driving."

Mrs. Graham was beginning to be a little disconcerted, she had by no means calculated on any opposition from David. When Lady Fordyce first told her, which she did with much less reluctance than she had shown to David, her wishes about their immediate union, she had felt quite elated; for the desire with her for her son's marriage was quite as great as it had been six months ago, and she had once or twice confided to Mr. Graham her fears, that after all their time, trouble, expense, and anxiety nothing would come of it, for Hilda certainly showed no predeliction for her intended husband. This sudden proposition, therefore, revived her hopes, and she meant to battle bravely on to succeed in bringing it to bear.

" Why, my dear son," said Mrs. Graham, mildly, " think of how short a time it is since Hilda was a mere child, and then take into consideration that you never attempt to conciliate her; however, David, she is young enough for you to mould her to your will."

A revengeful, bad expression passed over the face of the young man, they were true interpretations of his thoughts.

" Does Hilda know your wishes, Lady Fordyce ?" he asked, hurriedly.

" No, I would not say a word to her, till I had seen your mother and yourself."

" When do you wish our marriage should take place ?" he asked.

"On Monday morning, David, in this room. I dare not reckon on much time, and I fear to postpone it. I pray God will spare me to see you united, and to bless you both, and then my task is done; and I shall be ready to go to my Father in heaven, and pray Him to prosper you, as long as he sees fit to leave you here below."

David rose; he went up close to Lady Fordyce, and took her hand.

"I will make Hilda my wife if she consents. I will leave you now, for I shall not have much time to arrange all that must be done; and you can settle anything more you have to say with my mother, as I shall not be able to be here again till Monday morning."

Not saying another word, or waiting for a reply, he left the room, and went straight out of the house—but not home. The Park was not closed; he went in there, and sat down in a retired place, where he could think

over the step he was about to take in so
hurried and extraordinary a manner.

David Graham hated Hilda Chichester;
no other word could express his feeling.
Had he not done so, he would not have
consented to marry her.   He wanted to
humble her, to make her suffer for the way
in which she had treated him.   He did not
forget a single instance, or a single word that
she had annoyed him with.   He knew of
her attachment to Mr. Wentworth, he had
seen it from the commencement, and though
he never loved Hilda, he liked her sufficiently
to feel hatred to the man who had succeeded
in gaining her affections when he had failed;
perhaps it was his vanity hurt.

But he had long ceased to care for Hilda,
and, latterly, had disliked her.   Had Lady
Fordyce told him Hilda knew of her inten-
tions, he would have refused.   But he had
not found her in any great sorrow; he thought
he should have done so had she been made

acquainted with them; but had she known them, and still been happy, he would have gained nothing by it, and therefore, would have slipped out of it. Now, he had the hope of revenge—he should revenge himself on both of them, Walter and Hilda.

His reason for excusing himself from going again to Park Lane till the Monday, was to avoid meeting her. He hated scenes; besides, he thought she might, perhaps, appeal to him to release her, and from the first moment that the thought of revenge crossed his mind, it was too sweet to be relinquished.

There was a fiendish expression in his heavy, ill-natured face, that could Lady Fordyce have seen, as he was thinking over the misery he should cause, that would have made her rather have seen Hilda in her coffin, than his wife.

When David left, Lady Fordyce sent down for Hilda; she thought it right to ask her whether she would consent to marry him at once, and she preferred doing so whilst Mrs. Graham was with her. She could not entirely dispel a certain misgiving she had, as to whether she should be really securing all for Hilda by this hasty marriage she at first hoped. But she crushed it for the moment, and Mrs. Graham acted like an avalanche whilst by her side; she swept all doubts and fears bravely before her, and left nothing but the solid, firm impressions of good that they all had when it was first mooted at Burwood. She could expatiate, and with perfect sincerity, for she believed in them, on all David's amiable qualities. She promised that Hilda should be like her own child, that she loved her already, and she would love her more dearly still, for the sake of Lady Fordyce, and as David's wife. She told her she would at once give up her place to Hilda, she should be mistress, and everything that could be done to make her happy

should.   Mr. Graham, as Lady Fordyce
knew, was fond of her; they would both
welcome her as a daughter.

By the time Hilda came up, Mrs. Graham
had succeeded in making poor Lady Fordyce
perfectly happy and contented, and as anxious
as ever to fulfil all her schemes for poor
Hilda's misery.

None know, none can foresee the folly and
wretchedness of an ill-assorted marriage; it
may end but in sorrow, and happy if it is so;
it may end in disgrace, and the chances are
in favour of the latter.   How can a man be
supposed to remain in a house where he can
find no comfort, no peace, no quiet, and
above all, no companion.   If love be wanting on his part, he will not care whether they
exist or not, but had he his choice he would
prefer their absence, for then he could give
a plausible excuse for absenting himself, for
preferring his club, where he found all that
was wanting at home.

The wife is left to solitude and bitter re-
flections, and learns too soon that she can
find plenty who are willing to pity her, and
console her, and in time—and it does not
take a long time—constant neglect, with the
counterfeeling of others knowing it, will soon
produce the change, and God then only
knows what the end of that woman's state
will be.

If love be on the husband's side, and not
on the wife's, it is even worse than in the
other way.   For the man knows not how to
control his feelings as a woman can ; from
her childhood upwards, she has been taught
to disguise her love, and she has the wisdom
to do so, when it would satiate, perhaps, even
disgust.   A man cannot do this ; he, on the
contrary, gives way, and the repulsion he
meets, but adds fuel to fire.   He reproaches
her, she defends herself, till at last his love
for her dies, and they both seek in others'

society, what they cannot find in their own.

Hilda was in her aunt's room a very few minutes after she had sent for her; she had only waited to listen to the end of a remark her uncle was making, and to give a reply. She went up slowly, she knew her aunt was not alone, for she had asked John, and he had told her "Mr. David Graham had gone, but Mrs. Graham was still up-stairs." She felt very happy this evening, happier than she had been since the common gloom that had fallen on the whole household alike. She stopped at the drawing-room door for a moment, and went in; it looked dreary enough, but not to her eyes, for it was chiefly there she saw Walter, and though he was not there, everything seemed to remind her of some trifling word that was precious to her beyond expression.

She stood there as if in a pleasant dream, she looked at the balcony, where she recol-

ected the first words of love, the first embrace passed between them, and she pressed
her own hands against her lips, as if to feel
she was awake, that she was not dreaming;
that it was really true, that he did love her,
and that she had bright hopes now of becoming his wife; for her uncle, the only one
she would soon have to consult, was fond of
him, and she cared little who besides did, or
did not, like him.

He was to come to breakfast to-morrow,
would her uncle say anything to him then,
she thought; not just yet. And then she
wondered what he thought of her note—the
first she had ever written him—whether he
would prize it.

CHAPTER V.

IT was with a hopeful, though not joyous face, that Hilda entered the sick room, for she had felt a damp to her happiness on nearing her aunt's room; all her sufferings, and agony, and approaching death, all tended to sober down her wild, happy thoughts. But hope was there, strong within her, and would not entirely be hidden.

She went up, and kissed her as she always did, and Lady Fordyce, as she was moving away, held her hand, and looked steadily in her face.

Two minutes, at least, passed so, without a word being uttered.   At last, she said,

"Sit down close to me, my child, for I feel tired and weak; but yet I have something to ask you still."

"Leave it till to-morrow, auntie, it is late for you; let us go down and leave you to sleep, and I will come to you the first thing in the morning.   Won't it be better, Mrs. Graham?" said Hilda.

"If you really feel tired, dear Lady Fordyce, it might be more prudent for you to rest now," said Mrs. Graham, in a tone which said, as plainly as it could, "I think you ought to speak at once."

"I would rather do all I have to do to-night, and I shall sleep very much better when my mind is no longer burthened.   I told you, Hilda, I had a request to make, a prayer to ask of you, and I told you I should only ask it to-morrow.   It was because I thought I, perhaps, had a longer time to be with you, that I might have delayed it; but I find, dear, my days will be short, my hours few, and I have none to waste. Do not weep, darling, for it will unnerve me, and then I could not say all I wish. You told me, there was nothing you could do that you would not do for me. I blessed you for saying it, dear Hilda, and now it only remains for me to tell you what my entreaty is. It is Hilda—" she paused, for Hilda's face was turned up to hers, she had been leaning it against the side of the bed, and her large soft eyes were watching her aunt's face with deep earnestness; there was no longer that anxious look she had had before, when the promise was alluded to, it was calm and peaceful.

"Tell me what you wish, auntie dear, I am sure you will find me more than willing to do anything to please you."

"It is that you will let me leave you in the care and protection of your cousin David before I die—that you will give him a husband's right to protect you."

The words seem to fall upon Hilda's ear as if she were stone deaf, she neither moved nor spoke. And the only intimation of her having understood them, was the deathlike paleness that spread over her beautiful face.

Lady Fordyce put her hand gently on her arm and said, " You do not answer me, Hilda. Tell me, will you consent to grant me a happy, peaceful journey from this world to my everlasting home, in the next ?"

Hilda thus urged, merely said, " Impossible." She did not move, nor did the ghastly paleness diminish.

Lady Fordyce felt perplexed, she did not know exactly what her niece meant ; she could not see herself the expression on her face, for her head had fallen a little on her breast.

" What is impossible, darling ?" asked Lady Fordyce.

" It is impossible, aunt, that I should ever

become David Graham's wife," answered Hilda in a clear, firm tone; and her own words seemed to restore a little energy to her, for she looked up at her aunt, and there was something of Walter's stern expression in her eye as she did so.

"Oh, Hilda dear, don't say so, if you refuse—if you crush all my hopes for you thus, what will become of you? What shall I suffer at leaving you? Think, my child, think of the struggle you will cause me; think of the sorrow at seeing my fondest hopes dashed to the ground. Hilda, you will break my heart—you will kill me! then you will repent that you refused what I only asked for your own sake. Think of all the love I have expended on you, remember what I have done for you, what I still will do for you, and you know had God spared me what I would have done. Oh! then, in pity, Hilda, do not say it is impossible—do not send me to my grave broken-hearted. Pro-

mise—promise me, that on Monday morning
I may see you made man and wife."

Lady Fordyce gave here a cry of pain,
she had in her excitement moved herself,
and any motion caused her acute agony from
her internal injuries. She closed her eyes,
and the tears ran down her face.

"You cannot willingly, Hilda, inflict such
torture on one who has been such a friend to
you," said Mrs. Graham. "Look at her; if she
suffers so now, what will she do if you were to
persist—if she were to die now, you would
never have another happy moment as long as
life was granted you; you would reproach yourself unceasingly with being the cause—you
know shocks of any kind are injurious. Then
let your kind heart dictate to you, and then
follow its advice—I know it will tell you to
do what she wishes; and listen, dear Hilda,
there is nothing in life I will not do to make
you happy—there is nothing I will not willingly resign to you as David's wife. You

know Mr. Graham loves you as a daughter, you will find our affection will but increase for you. Think, then, well, Hilda, before you cause the unending sorrow you too surely will if you persist in this refusal."

Lady Fordyce had not opened her eyes since the pain had seized her. There was every now and then a stifled sob, and her chest was heaving.

Hilda watched her a minute, and then said in a low voice,

" Would it make you happy, aunt—would it relieve you were I to promise what you wish."

" Oh, Hilda, you do not know the joy— the unspeakable joy it would give me," and the poor sick woman turned to re-awake again to hope. " Look, can you refuse now, Hilda, when you see what even the mere shadow of expectation does."

" When did you say you wished it to be ?" asked Hilda.

"On Monday morning," said Mrs. Graham, "and your aunt wishes to see the ceremony performed, so it must be in this room."

Hilda rose up slowly, she gently kissed her aunt and said, "I will promise, aunt," and left the room.

She passed to her own, and as was her usual habit when she wished to be secure from the servants coming in, locked her door. There are many kinds of sorrows—many ways of suffering from it. Some can weep in intense grief, their tears relieve them; they seem by degrees to wash the sharpness of it off, it is a vent for it, they gradually become soothed and calmed. Others can talk of their sorrow, they can discuss it and linger on it, and feel the better for having unburthened themselves. Some are violent, and rave and rant, and declare it is impossible to live, they must put an end to their existence; they neither eat, drink, nor sleep, but those who are so affected, recover the first, the very violence of their mourning is its own cure.

But some neither weep, nor talk, nor are violent, and it is those who truly suffer, and who know what real grief is, and of that number was Hilda. She would have died if she could, she wished to do so; but the idea of taking her own life never crossed her mind, she had been taught to fear and love God, and therefore to rush into his presence uncalled, would never have suggested itself to her. There was a cold heavy pain at her heart, she pressed her hand against it, for it almost choked her; her temples throbbed, and she scarcely could tell what the dull aching misery came from.

But when the thought of David as her husband rose before her, she shut her eyes as if she feared she might see him then, and a cold shudder ran through her whole frame. She loathed the very thought of him, how then could she ever bring herself to be his wife. It did indeed seem impossible. How could she ever swear to love and honour him, when she hated him, despised him ; and yet she had passed her word to take that solemn oath before God, and what or who was there to save her. She was bewildered in her misery, but not a tear fell, she suffered in silence with nothing to alleviate her. She clasped her hands in agony, but she sat otherwise perfectly still. The paleness that overspread her face, when in her aunt's room, had returned, and she looked like a beautiful statue, but with such utter woe depicted on her countenancee, that it would have made one weep to look at.

Hilda could not realize to herself David as her husband. It was impossible she could live with him—impossible for her to be condemned to be his constant companion—impossible for her to receive his caresses ; she shuddered as that thought came with others.

For she knew what it was to love with all her heart and soul, she knew what it was to be loved; but at that moment she did not think of that, it merely crossed her thoughts without her knowing it.

Had she not loved Walter, the probability is, she would have married David without repulsion, though without love; but from the time of her attachment to Walter, her endurance, for it scarcely ever amounted to more, of David, gradually subsided, till nothing was now left but dislike, amounting to hatred.

There was a knock at the door; but she heard nothing, nothing but the beating of her own heart. It was repeated a second time very loudly, and some one tried to open the door; she turned her head towards it for a moment, and then back again, as if it did not matter to her. But the third time it roused her, for the door was shaken, and the knocking continued. She rose and opened it.

"Dear me, Miss, how you did frighten me, to be sure; I have been knocking and knocking, and calling this I don't know how long. Here is a note for you if you please, Miss."

And Strange disappeared, and Hilda re-locked the door. She was in the dark, so she could not see who the letter was from, she laid it down, and began to think again, though it was scarcely to be called thinking, all seemed so imaginary. At length she went to her little writing-table, and struck a light, she thought it must be late, and if she could sleep and so lose recollection even for a few hours it would be a blessing; but it was only half-past nine, so she knew she would be presently summoned to tea, she had forgotten it till then, she hoped to avoid seeing anyone to-night.

Her eye fell on the unopened letter before her, she took it up, the envelope was sealed by initials that took her little time to de-cipher—W. W. entwined. She opened it hastily, it was to her like a drop of water to a being dying from thirst. She read as follows :

"Friday night, C— Club.

"You do not know, my own dearest Hilda, the joy your few lines gave me, the first I have ever received from you. Tell Sir William, should he ask whether I sent an answer, that I will be *chez lui* at nine punctually to-morrow morning, and if I find my darling down five minutes earlier, she

will be sure to find some one waiting for
her.

"W. WENTWORTH."

She read it and re-read it, she kissed it,
she for a few minutes forgot her sorrow
and basked in the sunshine of his love.
She pressed it to her bosom, she paced up
and down her room grasping it, as if she
thought some one was coming to snatch
it from her. She hugged it to her, as a
mother would her child she thought some
wild beast was going to tear from her.
Why had she not thought of Walter before?
What had made her think of marrying
David when Walter was there to claim
her? He would protect her, he would
guard her, he would shield her from such
a calamity as becoming David's wife.
Oh, what joy entered her soul! more

intense from the sorrow she had under-gone.

How she longed for the morning, how she longed to tell him all, how she longed to hear his voice reassure and comfort her; grief had left her, except the traces it had left upon her cheeks.

CHAPTER VI.

WHEN Lady Fordyce and Mrs. Graham were left alone, there was an evident restraint between them. It was hardly possible for the one not to feel she had been consenting and aiding to the blighting the whole life of a young and beautiful girl, for the sake of gratifying her own selfish wishes, and pandering to those of a dying woman ; whilst the latter, in her blind ignorance, thought, if Hilda did not like the prospect of marrying David now, it would be very different when she was once his wife. Her whole feelings would change towards him. Yes, Lady Fordyce was quite correct in what she said—that her whole feelings would change—they would, but not in the way she meant, they would become ten times more bitter; he would be still more hateful and abhorrent to her. His very presence would cause her inmost feelings to revolt.

Let no young girl delude herself, or be deluded into thinking that love will come after marriage. Never, never, unless there be a sound, firm, foundation of respect or esteem with which a woman, if her heart be free, may safely build a fortress strong enough to risk her future happiness, and she may, if of a well disciplined mind, easily learn to love the man who is deserving of her best opinion. But let her not think that a marriage formed without these firm bases can ever stand a few

months, and the fair fine edifice will be but
a crumbled ruin. It is strange how parents,
guardians, and all who have any power, still
persist daily to instil into the minds of those
they have authority over, the same argument,
if it happens to be an alliance they think
advisable, and where the woman feels her
heart in no way concerned.

It is a good match, and so she is sure to
be very fond of him after a time. He is a
capital catch, so love must soon grow between them. It matters not if he is an ill-
principled, irreligious man—he is rich and a
first-rate *partie*; young men will sow their
wild oats, it won't do for fathers and brothers
to be severe, it might so happen that they
are birds of a feather. But be that as it
may, a good match in England, or indeed
anywhere, is not to be thrown aside
simply because a foolish, silly girl can-

not make up her mind to fall in love with him.

No, let her marry, and she will soon love him. And she does marry—then, too late, fathers, mothers and brothers are surprised that Mary's or Jane's marriage had turned out so unfortunately, he was a good fellow, and she was a nice, pretty girl, and both are wretched; both have a long weary life before them, tied together, yet more apart than the most distant acquaintances, both condemning the other, both wrong, and so doomed for life. Yes, for life—does it enter a girl's head when she is going to be married that it *is* for life, as long as they both shall live— that nothing but crime on the one side or the other can sever them, and then they succeed from misery to disgrace—disgrace to the woman of the blackest, deepest dye—a disgrace that shuts her out from communion with her own sex, that closes every door against her.

And who is the primary and chief cause of this? Who but those who told her, and whom she implicitly believed, that she would love the man she herself thought she should never like, when she became his wife—when she found herself entirely thrown upon him, for society, for advice, for sympathy, for protection, for all, in short, that a woman ought to find in her husband, but so rarely does.

Parents, and those in the place of parents, have much, very much to answer for to their God, for the way they perform their duty to those placed under their care, not when they are children, but later in life, when instead of thinking of their good, they consider their own.

"Do you not think Hilda seems very much opposed to so sudden a marriage?"

asked Lady Fordyce, she did not like to say
that she thought it was the individual more
than the fact she objected to, for fear of
hurting Mrs. Graham's feelings; she hesitated to do that to a person she liked, as being
an old friend, and yet she willingly rent all
the tenderer feelings of the one she loved best
in the world, to gratify a fancy of her
own.

"No, no more than any girl would be;
there is always a natural shrinking on such
occasions," said Mrs. Graham, "which of
course you and I are too sensible to notice."

"Well, but," said Lady Fordyce, who was
anxious to be persuaded out of her doubts,
" that would not cause her to have said it was
impossible; and she was so silent and quiet,
and seemed so calm, it was not timidity
that."

" I really think, dear Lady Fordyce, that

had you and I at seventeen been told suddenly on one day, we were to be married within forty-eight hours, to a man scarcely looked on as a lover, it would have startled us a little; and there is no accounting in what manner different people are moved under different circumstances. Hilda is naturally a very quiet, unexciteable person, she does not show her feelings, so I am not at all surprised at the manner she received your request in; indeed it was exactly what I thought and expected."

"But did you not hear her say that she could never become David's wife?" again asked Lady Fordyce, delighted at finding all her misgivings being dispersed one by one.

"My dear Lady Fordyce, you surely can think nothing of that, when within ten minutes afterwards she promised to be his wife in two days time. She may have thought for the moment that David had acted so little like a lover, that he may have impressed her as not being fond enough of her."

" Does David not care for her; because what misery have I been laying the foundation for if he is not attached to her."

" David loves Hilda, believe me, more than he ever loved any other girl," replied Mrs. Graham, this time thinking she spoke the truth; and it would have been so if she had said it three months earlier, for David rather liked Hilda, and had never even endured any one else, so there was little doubt of the latter part of her speech.

" I should have been surprised had he not, for I cannot imagine any one not liking my pretty gentle Hilda. She will make a loving good wife, for she has been a good, I might almost say a daughter to me; I never had a moment's anxiety about her, she was always obedient, submissive and yielding."

" I do not wish to take from or diminish merits, but remember, dear Lady Fordyce, you never opposed or thwarted her in any single instance," said Mrs. Graham.

" Only because there was no occasion ; she was naturally good, and so truthful, I don't think she knows what a falsehood is ; I never knew her deviate a hair's breadth from the pure straightforward truth, it is one of the most beautiful traits in her character. Don't think me influenced in my opinion of her by my affection, for I am not—she is all I tell you, she is as near perfection as a young girl can be. You must tell David all this, he left so soon, and I shall not see him till Monday ; and it will come better from you than from me, he will think me partial. I wish it were over ; it makes me restless and uneasy, and

now it is fixed, I fear whether I may even be
spared so long, for I feel something over me
as if my time was fast drawing near. They
say the flame brightens before the candle
goes out, and so it is with me. I have,
through God's mercy, been enabled to settle
and arrange all this during the day, and I
could not have done it any time since my
calamity. But I feel very tired now, and
my head aches. You will see Hilda as you
go down, and tell her to send Sir William to
me, and talk to her a little, and should you
notice anything, or should she say anything
that would lead you to think she is opposed
to her marriage, beyond what you say is
natural, you will tell me, and now I will say
good night to you."

She did look tired, and there was a black
and hollow look round her eyes that gave her
a worn, languid appearance.

On going down, Mrs. Graham only found
Sir William, he had just had an interview
with the doctor, who had called to enquire
how his patient was ; and he told Sir William he could not tell from day to day which
would be her last, but he doubted her linger-
ing on till Monday ; he told Sir William of
her desire to know, and his reply, but he
thought it right in case it might be of importance to let him know what he really believed.

Sir William did not think it necessary
to tell Mrs. Graham ; he was not naturally
communicative, and it had depressed him
a great deal ; his poor wife had lived so
many days longer than was at first thought
possible after her accident, that he almost
forgot that the time she would be spared
could but amount to a few days ; and yet
it is always the case under such events,

the blow falls almost as keenly at last as if it had never been anticipated.

Mrs. Graham asked for Hilda, and was told she had not been down since her aunt sent for her; so' she went upstairs to look for her. She went to her room and knocked; this time it was opened with alacrity, and Hilda's face was again peaceful and happy, and Walter's letter still in her hand.

" Oh, it is you, Mrs. Graham, does auntie want me ?"

" No, dear, she is tired and does not wish to be disturbed again to-night; but she begged me to see you before I went."

" Shall we go down to tea ?" said Hilda, " I am sure you must be starving, for 1 don't believe you have had any dinner; but you shall have a substantial tea if you will stop."

" No, thank you, Hilda, I will go home as soon as I have spoken to you for a few minutes. You distressed your aunt very much by your manner, she feared all sorts of impossible things till I quieted her by assuring her all her fears were imaginary. Try and re-assure her yourself, my dear, for I am sure you would not willingly cause her any uneasiness on your account."

"I am glad, dear Mrs. Graham, to be able to speak to you on the subject, for my aunt was quite right in her ideas, if they were that my objections to becoming your son's wife are insurmountable. You do not imagine that they arise from any foolish childish fancies I am sure. Believe me they are good reasons and strong ones, and I regret deeply I led my aunt to believe I would fulfil her wishes, it was very wrong in me to promise, for I cannot perform it. And you will help me, Mrs. Graham, will you not, to point out to my aunt that it will not tend to either my happiness or David's, that we are not suited to each other. I am quite sure he would deeply and for ever repent such a step."

"Stop, Hilda," cried Mrs. Graham, "you wrong David, and you misjudge me, if you think he is not proud to make you his wife, or if you expect me to be the medium of breaking the marriage, for two reasons—it would be causing my son's happiness to be destroyed, and I believe it would kill your aunt."

Hilda's heart was beginning to sink within her, but she felt Walter's letter in her hand, she grasped it tighter and tighter, and felt her courage rise ; after all it little mattered whether Mrs. Graham would or would not endeavour to save her and her son from utter misery, she would do it herself, and she felt she should succeed.

"I am sorry, Mrs. Graham, if I pained you by what I said, but it is better to be open on a matter interesting one's whole life; and I am quite sure I never could make David happy, and I feel I do not sufficiently love him to become his wife."

"You did not think so when you were at Burwood," said Mrs. Graham, "you then were willing enough to consent to your aunt's wishes; and yet now on her death-bed, you deliberately refuse the only request she makes you, though she tells you that if you refuse it will cause her to leave this world with a weight of care and sorrow, that few dis-interested people would like to feel they had occasioned, much less one on whom she has lavished all the fondness and tenderness of a mother. You scarcely can persevere in such ingratitude when you think of it in this light. Supposing even you did not like

David, that he was personally objectionable to you, you would but sacrifice a momentary feeling of your own for the sake of granting to your poor dying aunt all the happiness and peace of mind she can ever have. You can actually feel that you have it in your power to do this, and yet you can sacrifice her on her death-bed, to a foolish ridiculous notion that you do not love David sufficiently; and so you would render her end bitter and sad, you for whom she thought nothing in life a sacrifice."

"But I think," said poor Hilda, nearly overcome by Mrs. Graham's words, "if my aunt knew how much I dislike the idea, she would not hold to it so much. If she did not think it would tend to my happiness, she would no longer desire it."

"You are wrong in supposing so; she would still desire it as intensely as she does now, perhaps even more. But I cannot now reason any longer with you, it is getting very late, and I must go home. I can only pray, Hilda, for your own sake, and for your future peace of mind, that you say nothing hastily or thoughtlessly to your aunt, for I believe her to be much nearer death than you or your uncle seem to think; and remember, did she die from over-excitement, or any shock to her nervous system, you would never have another peaceful or happy moment, as long as you lived."

And with that consoling remark, she left Hilda to reflect on all she had said.

Her uncle sent for her as soon as Mrs. Graham was gone. He had been up to Lady Fordyce, but she was too worn out for him to say more than wish her good night. He was not sorry, for he shrunk, as most men do, from harrowing his feelings unnecessarily, and seeing and talking to her, after hearing that any hour might be her last, would have been very painful.

Hilda was very glad to go to her uncle; she would tell him what had passed, and hear his opinion, though she half dreaded finding it would agree with her aunt's and Mrs. Graham's; but the remembrance of his smile, on seeing her note to Walter, and his telling her he was glad, re-assured her a little.

He was sitting in the back drawing-room. Tea was on the table, and the lamps lighted. It looked comfortable and pleasant, but he was sitting with a hand on each knee, and his eyes as if fixed on some object very distant.

" What is the matter, uncle?" said Hilda, going up to him, " are you not well, or are you tired of waiting for your tea? And

here are the evening papers, and you have
not opened them even."

She tried to speak cheerfully, but she felt
sad enough ; but she generally forgot her
own sorrows, when she came in contact with
others' grief, notwithstanding Mrs. Graham's
accusation of selfishness against her.

"I have been dreadfully upset, Hilda,
and you will be as pained as I am when
I tell it to you. It seems so dreadful—so
awful !"

"What is it, dear uncle ? Surely no
more sorrow for us ! We have had enough
lately," said Hilda.

"Mr. Hancock came to me this evening,
and told me, as he considered it his duty to
do, that—" Sir William got up and walked
to the window, which was still open ; he
drew his handkerchief across his eyes, and
then turning back to Hilda, continued,

" that her hours are numbered, and I must be prepared at any moment to lose her. She asked Hancock herself this afternoon what he thought, but he merely told her if she were anxious to arrange anything not to delay it; so she is quite conscious of it. Poor Mary !" and her uncle walked up and down the room.

Hilda had sat down on the sofa whilst her uncle was talking, and now her face was buried in the cushion. If her aunt should die before Monday, she would be saved, but the thought no sooner crossed her mind, than she hated herself for it.

Was it possible she could be so bad, so heartless, so unfeeling, that the idea of her aunt's death could be looked to as a sort of release to herself. The aunt she so loved, so revered ; so fond, so good to her. No; she even, for the moment, hoped she might live, that she might prove she could and would sacrifice herself for her sake.

She determined to say nothing to Sir William to-night, she would wait to the next day, it would be quite time enough; and she would tell her aunt the first thing the following morning she would marry David, to prove how she loved her, and that she would do anything she wished, and anything that would make her mind easy.

But as before, when Hilda gave her aunt the promise, she did not think of Walter. It was not till she was in her own room that she recollected him. She again read his letter, and once more all her good resolves were dashed to the ground. She could battle strongly enough when she thought of herself only, but when she thought of him, she was weak and powerless;

and she once more decided on leaving it in his hands, and for him to guide and direct her.

CHAPTER VII.

WHAT an aching, miserable feeling one has in the morning on first awaking after having had some sorrow over-night. We awake, we feel there is something that has left a weight on our hearts, but, for the moment, we cannot recollect what it is, and then suddenly it flashes across the mind, and it is harder to bear from the momentary forgetfulness we enjoyed.

It was so with Hilda on the Saturday morning. She felt an oppression and heaviness that at first she could not account for, but the cause soon discovered itself. She buried her face in the pillow as if she would shut it out.

In the morning, everything is more clear, more apparent, more easy of comprehension, and more true; we see facts as they are. At night, we see them as we wish them to be, and generally, darkness seems to influence and bias our way of viewing them. In the morning, solitude and daylight wonderfully alter the phase of things.

Hilda could no longer view her position so hopefully as she did the night previous. She no longer felt anxious, or even willing, to sacrifice herself to her aunt's wishes. She remembered Walter was to be there before nine, and she hurried to be dressed in time to see him, as he had asked.

She first went into Lady Fordyce's room. She was still sleeping, so Hilda did not disturb

her. As she watched her, she remembered
what her uncle told her last night, and she
felt her heart swell within her. She felt it
was an awful thing to watch one so calmly
and peacefully asleep, and to know that so
soon she would sleep the long, long sleep of
death.

As she stood there in that room, which
death seemed already to have taken possession of—it was so still—all her young life
rose before her; she remembered her father
dying when she was little more than a baby.
She then followed events as they occurred till
she first saw Walter. It was then her life
truly began, or, at all events, the interest of
it. She cared for little now, compared with
him, he had woven himself into her very
soul, her whole life would be a blank without his love. What then was to become
of another man's wife, when the very

thought of him would be a sin. God help her !

She was roused by hearing something drive up and stop at their door. She gently left her aunt's room, and went down stairs. Walter had just come in, and was in the small room which Sir William and Hilda had made their dining-room, since there had been but themselves to occupy it. It was a pretty morning room, but at the back of the house, so did not look over the Park.

Walter had taken up the ' Times,' and was reading it when Hilda went in.

" Always that horrid paper, Walter, the first thing in the morning," said Hilda, smiling, " I often wonder what you and my uncle find so attractive in it that you can spell it over as you do."

" Good morning, my little scold, is that all

you have to say to me, after my turning out at this unearthly hour to have a few minutes' quiet glimpse of you all to myself. But my darling looks sad—what is the matter with you? Your aunt is the same, I suppose. You must cheer up and look happy when I am with you, or I shall think the sight of me is enough to make you *triste*."

"Oh, Walter, I have somewhat to look sad about; but you know, if any one in the world could make me look or feel happier, it is yourself."

"Why, Hilda, what is it? If I can do anything, you know you have but to ask me, and I would think anything a pleasure that would dispel the gloom on your dear face. Come and sit by me, my own, and tell me what is distressing you," and he drew her gently towards him, and placed her by his side on the ottoman.

For a moment she laid her head on his shoulder, and the tears fell slowly down her pale cheeks.

" Why, Hilda, you must not give way so ! Where is all your bravery gone to ? I thought you could weather any storm. But tell me at once, dearest, for Sir William will be coming in soon, and then, adieu to my hearing your grievance !"

" Oh, Walter, you make light of it, but that is because you do not know what it is."

" And I am not likely to, you dolorous little lady, if you don't make haste and tell me; besides, I am curious," said Walter, smiling.

" You have heard, Walter, that last Christmas, when the Grahams were staying with us at Burwood—it was the same time you were asked and refused—they were very anxious that I should marry their son ? You have heard all about it before, haven't you?" said Hilda, with her eyes fixed on the floor.

Walter was silent for a moment, and when he replied, it was in his stern firm voice, not like the same person who had just been talking. " I have heard some indirect remarks about it, but as you never alluded to it in speaking to me, I of course gave the story no more credit than most London gossip deserves."

Hilda was puzzled, she did not know whether Walter was angry or vexed; she felt afraid to go on, yet unless she told him all, how could he advise or guide her.

"You must not be angry with me, Walter," she said, her voice quivering, "I thought so little of the matter, and considered it of so little importance that I did not think there was any use in telling you, though I so often wished to do so; but you never alluded to it in any way to give me the opportunity, and I thought you might wonder why I troubled you about such a foolish affair."

Walter liked to see her as she was now, in a kind of submissive mood, and as if she dreaded displeasing him; he knew the power his look and tone of voice had over her, and he liked to feel how completely she was under his influence.

"If you still wish to tell me, I will listen," he replied coldly.

"No," she replied, rising, a slight colour mounting to her cheeks, though the tears were yet in her eyes, her voice was firm. "I have no right to trouble you, nor any right to claim either your advice, or counsel, on matters in which you, I see, have no interest."

She was going to the bell to ring it, but
Walter jumped up and holding her back, said,
" What are you going to do, Hilda?"

" Merely order breakfast," she answered
carelessly.

" No, you will sit down again, tell me what
you intended, and you must remember if
I appeared annoyed, it is not pleasant for me
to hear other men's names coupled with
yours. But what is it about this cousin of
yours, and what can there be to worry you
about him now? Come, Hilda, you must
not be angry," he said, as she still seemed
inclined to rebel against his efforts to recon-
cile her. " I shall think you do not love me,
as you told me you did, if you are so easily
vexed. Look at me, Hilda, and let me read
in your eyes the truth, for they cannot
deceive me," he raised her face, so she could
not help looking at him, his own eyes were

looking so fondly at her, that she felt all her anger melt away.

He was quite aware how far he could go with her, for he knew her pride was great, that it required a little management to bring her round if he had put her out; he knew her character better than he knew his own, though they resembled each other very much.

" Now I am forgiven, so you need not pretend any more resentment, and you must seal your pardon," and he stooped down and pressed his lips to hers. Hilda gave way for the moment to all the intensity of her love for him, and returned his embrace with more tenderness than he had ever known her do before; but it was not long she could enjoy her happiness, sad bitter thoughts came in rapid succession.

" Oh, Walter, I will tell you ; but I must

do so quickly, for we shall not have very much time, and if I don't tell you now, perhaps I may never be able." She put one of her hands in his, as they were again sitting side beside each other.

"It appears that Mr. and Mrs. Graham were so anxious I should marry David, that they did what they could not make up their minds to do before, they came to London to remain the season, so that they might manage it before I was presented, or been out at all. When my uncle and aunt heard they were coming to town—they said it was to consult a physician for Mrs. Graham—they begged them to stop at Burwood a few weeks beforehand. They came, and soon after they were there, my aunt sent for me, and told me it was the wish of them all that I should become David's wife, and she asked me if I had any dislike to it. I had known David

when I was quite a child, when we went to
Scotland every year, and he was always good-
natured to me, and though I did not care
much about him, I did not dislike him.
So I told my aunt, if she wished it, I did not
care one way or the other. She was very
pleased, and they all seemed so. It was
arranged by my aunt there should be no
engagement, that I should be quite free till
this July, but that then, if I still consented,
we were to be married.

"I saw very little of him at Burwood, he
but once spoke to me on the subject, in an
off-hand, indifferent manner; but from the
moment it seemed settled, I felt sad and
sorry the idea had ever been thought of. I
used to think of you, Walter," she said, looking up at him with such deep tenderness in
her beautiful eyes. "I used to compare you,
and by degrees I began to dislike David for

being so unlike everything you were. All, every thought became about you; I longed to see you again, and you do not know the disappointment I felt when you declined coming; and then when we came to town, my only wish was to see you, so that I might be quite sure you were what I thought you. I was afraid I should see you like David."

"My darling, and did I possess your heart then?"

"Yes, dear Walter, but that has nothing to do with what I have to tell," she replied innocently. "I soon learnt you were all I fancied you, and very very soon I forgot all about David and what passed at Burwood. I seldom saw him, and each time I did, I learnt to like him less and love you more. I never thought again about him, till my brother Arthur, on the night of our ball, told me to remember I was David's affianced wife, and that my conduct as such was improper. I was beginning to defend myself, when Lord Borton interrupted us to ask me to dance. I told him I was engaged, Arthur asked me who to, and I said to you; he wished me to promise not to dance with you again, I refused, and then you came for me—you know what followed."

Walter pressed her to him, and said, " I do, Hilda, we were happy, very happy that night, but go on."

" I determined," she continued, " the first opportunity to tell my aunt that I considered it time she should know I never could and never would be David's wife. I did so on the Sunday of her fatal accident. She was very grieved and pained, and almost reproached me for my want of gratitude for all her love for me, and told me I should break her heart if I persisted; it ended in my telling her I would do anything she wished. There of course the matter rested, till last night, and then, Walter, before Mrs. Graham, whom she had sent for, she implored me to become his wife immediately, that she might bless me as such before she died. She said, if I refused, I should cause her death-bed a pang that I never should forgive myself for. I told her it was impossible, but she did not seem to understand me; and, Walter, before I left her last night, 1 told her on Monday morning, the time that had been fixed between her and David, I would fulfil her wishes. I went to my own room, and your note was given to me; the agony and sorrow I was suffering seemed all to vanish at the recollection that I had you to advise and help me. But then came Mrs. Graham, and I appealed to her also to spare her son, if she would not for my sake, the unending sorrow such a marriage would entail; but she was firm in refusing, and again pointed out to me the awful consequences it might produce on my aunt, were I to continue in my refusal. She told me I should bring a curse upon me if I behaved with such ingratitude, and again I felt in the midst of a stormy sea, with no help near to save me. And added to this, Mr. Hancock came last night to tell my uncle he must be prepared at any moment for my poor aunt's end, and I feel perfectly bewildered, with fear and remorse on one side, and everlasting misery worse far than death, on the other. What shall I do, Walter?" and she crossed her face with her hands; she could not look at him, she felt as if she had been asking him to marry her. She wished she could explain to him she did not mean that, for she had not thought it appeared in that light till she heard her own

voice tell her tale. She wished she had
thought of it, she never would have told him
at all. But it was done now, she could not
unsay her words ; but she could tell him if he
were to say anything about himself, that she
had not thought more than of asking his
advice. She forgot she could have asked
her uncle instead of him, but it was just
as well, it would only have added to her
troubles.

When she had ceased speaking, Walter
got up and paced up and down the room;
he was perplexed and confused; he had not
been prepared for this ; it seemed to him as
if he was cruelly placed, as if there was no
opening of any kind but what would lead to
storms and difficulties. How could he
advise her, what could he say? why had she
gone to him, and so fixed him as to make
him either the cause of condemning her to a

life long misery worse than death, or him to inevitable ruin; there was no middle course, and still worse there was no time to alter the bent of purposes.

He could not tell her to marry David Graham, knowing her very heart and soul were his. How could he say he would take her to himself, to cherish and protect as long as he lived. If he did, he should seal his own doom. He knew he did not love her sufficiently to sacrifice himself for her; he knew though he felt now even unhappy about her, that when once he was gone from her, and no longer under the influence her beauty to a certain extent always had over him, he would repent, he had better withstand any step that would involve him in a promise of marriage. He wished Sir William would come in, and so for the moment put off his reply; or if he could in any way defer it till he had seen

Munro. Why had he not followed his advice and kept entirely out of her way; why, instead of seeking her, had he not avoided her, he might have foreseen that some evil would ensue from the course he followed.

"Sir William wishes breakfast to be at half-past nine, if you please, Miss," said John, opening the door.

Walter felt now there was no help for him, an hour more before he could hope for their tête-à-tête to be ended, and during that time he must speak, he must say something to comfort her.

The servant coming in had roused Hilda, and she said to Walter,

"You don't speak; will you not tell me how you think I should act? Perhaps I expressed myself badly—you may have misunderstood me in asking your advice, I thought you would tell me what you think it right for me to do, that is all I wish to know."

"No, Hilda, I have not misunderstood you, but you ask me to do an almost impossible thing. You ask me, an interested person, to give you disinterested advice—you ask me to tell you whether it is right to marry a man you dislike, when I know that you—"

"Well, Walter, go on, I know what you would say, it is very true; perhaps I ought not to have asked you, but last night the thought of having you to apply to made me feel so much happier, that it made me selfish, and I forgot in doing so I might pain you."

"Were I to tell you," said Walter, "that I thought it would be better for you to risk causing your aunt sorrow, rather than entail so much on yourself, what reason could you give for having changed again."

" What but the true one, that I don't esteem or like David, and never can do so," replied Hilda.

" Yes, but I doubt your aunt accepting that as a sufficient one; she would tell you you were too young to judge your feelings."

" Oh, she could not say that, for then, Walter, I could tell her I loved you, and have done so ever since I first saw you," answered Hilda.

This was what Walter feared, he feared if she were pressed on the point she would own her love for him as innocently as she had done to himself, and then he knew what must be the result of that, even should they accept that as sufficient excuse, and break off the marriage on account of it. The more he thought of it, the less did he like compromising himself in any way.

"Were you to do so, you would make everything in a worse state than it is; for were they still to insist on your marrying, you would place it in the power of Mr. Graham and his family to taunt you for ever for such an admission. You would make them your enemies, and render your future prospects more dark and more dreary than they even are now. On that point I can advise you, and let nothing induce you to own to a human being that you have ever thought more of me than any mere acquaintance. You have an enemy already in Mrs. Phillips, and depend upon it she will never lose an opportunity of doing you any injury she can —she is jealous of you. I have heard over and over again remarks she has made about you, full of ill-nature and spite. Never place

yourself in any one's power, you are sure to
repent it sooner or later."

Hilda thought Walter argued sensibly, but
not in the way she liked; he spoke to her as
if she were nothing more than an old friend
asking his opinion, not as the woman he had
professed to love—and after all, as yet he
had not helped her in any way, she was not
a bit nearer the point than when she had
been thinking it over in her own room. She
knew Matilda disliked her, she knew she
never lost an occasion of doing her any un-
kindness she could, but she cared little for
that or for her.

"I will tell you," said Walter suddenly,
"what I think you might do. Appeal to
your cousin himself, point out to him the
misery it will bring upon you, and upon him,
too; ask him, as you fail to do so, to try and
persuade Lady Fordyce that it will not tend

to your happiness. Tell him you do not love him, and if he be a man in anything but name, he will succeed in freeing you from such a mad affair."

"Yes, I can do that, and will. I will send for him this morning. Oh, I am so glad you have thought of it," said Hidla, as the idea seemed to increase in her estimation. "If I tell him all that, he must be inhuman if he does not help me. Thank you, dear Walter, for the suggestion, it all seems clear now. I am so thankful."

"So am I, dearest, if I have brought a smile back to your poor pale face ; it makes my heart ache to see you look so sad."

"You don't know what I have suffered, it seems like a dreadful dream, but I shall hope on now, and I shall owe all to you. I felt sure you would think of something, see some loop-hole, I could not."

But Walter was not so sanguine, though he was thankful the thought had suggested itself. He much feared David would not willingly resign the power of possessing poor Hilda, the fact of her dislike to him, would, to a selfish man like him, but add and increase his desire—opposition and difficulty in attaining an object always increases its value, and much more when as in the present case. But Walter had gained his end, and that was to take care of himself.

Sir William joined them very soon, he scarcely spoke, and evidently was preoccupied by his own thoughts, which to judge from his countenance, were none of the happiest. Walter asked him in what he could be of use to him, but he seemed to have forgotten all about his request to see him. It was not till Walter said something about his wish for him to be there early, and that he

had come in consequence, that he remembered he wanted him, if he could spare time,
to go down to Mitcham to his lawyer,
who had gone for a couple of days to
breathe the fresh air, instead of completing
his cure in London smoke. He wanted him
to come up and see Lady Fordyce by her
own desire.

Walter was very glad of the commission.
He wished to be absent whilst Hilda got
through her interview with David, and he
was glad to have a little time to try and
collect his thoughts.

It was a heavy, uncomfortable breakfast,
they each felt a restraint, that the others did
not understand. Sir William had been with
his wife, and she had told him her wishes
respecting Hilda, and of her interview first
with David and subsequently with Hilda,

and of both having consented to conform to her desires.

He had felt more grieved than it was well possible to consider why. But he had been influenced by circumstances very much in the same way Hilda had. He had no longer been anxious about Hilda's marriage with David, because he no longer liked David personally; he had compared him with Walter Wentworth during the last week or two. The one had been kindness and attention itself, the other had been the same rough, uncouth, unfeeling being he had always been. And then, it was but the night previous that he had built a very different castle in the air for Hilda. He could not understand her either. How could she promise to marry David, if, as he thought, she preferred Walter ?

But he thought silence would be the safest

course to adopt, he would not broach the subject if she did not. Perhaps, after all, she had refused Walter, and then he could only pain her by alluding to him in any way.

Most people think silence is always safe; in some few instances it may be, but as a rule, it is far safer to speak one's thoughts. Were it done more frequently, what heart-aches would be spared, what anxiety would be saved. How often do we not wish we could know each other's thoughts. Even were they to pain us, it would be better to know the worst at once. The longer the deception, the more bitter becomes the truth. We think people like us for ourselves, we find, after giving our best heart's feelings, that, after all, it is either our money or position is the attraction.

Yes, I wish the mind was a sheet of paper,

visible to the eye, that every thought would, as it passed over, be stamped on in legible characters.

Had Sir William Fordyce spoken, had he told Hilda what he thought, how the whole current of her future life might have been changed ! Or, had Hilda told him openly all she had endured, all she was enduring, she might yet have saved herself. She would have done so the previous evening, but fate interfered ; she thought it would seem selfish in her then to speak of herself, and so they both, from good motives, unconsciously worked ill to each other.

Soon after Walter had left, Mrs. Phillips came. She came daily, never more welcome one day than another. She invariably wanted something each day. One time it was the loan of the carriage ; another, a few bottles of Sir William's very best port ; a third time, the use of her mother's black lace shawl, the weather was so warm, and that she quite forgot to return. Once it was the pattern of one of her most beautiful bracelets, that a friend of hers wished to have one like. That, of course, was not remembered till some time after her poor mother's death, when Sir William could not find it anywhere, and on Hilda telling him Matilda had it, he asked her for it. She cried, and said it was very hard to take from her the only souvenir of her mother's that she really valued.

So he let her keep it, rather than be worried himself by hearing her talk, or seeing her face distorted, if possible, into a more ugly form than nature had already shaped it.

A small, thin, spare Frenchman, with a bristly moustache, once remarked on seeing her enter a room tolerably well filled, " Mon Dieu! cette femme s'est abusée de la permission que la nature lui a donnée d'être laide."

She went up to Lady Fordyce's room, and it was with undisguised joy she heard of Hilda's marriage. She thought Hilda ought to be unboundedly grateful. She was the most fortunate girl she had ever heard of, and she only feared she was not deserving of so much happiness.

Her mother intimated that Hilda did not seem at all over-elated, and that, on the contrary, she seemed to be rather against it, at least, had been at first.

"That is only her double-dealing ways, mamma, I always told you how deceitful she was. It only would require you to say you had changed your mind, to see whether she was pleased or not, though I don't advise you to try it, because David might not be so easily put off," said Mrs. Phillips, speaking so loudly that her mother closed her eyes, as if that would save her ears, poor woman.

In the course of that morning, Hilda sent a message to request David would call as soon as possible, as she wished to see him. The servant returned with the reply that Mr. David Graham regretted he should not be able to call in Park Lane at all during the day, as he should be engaged till very late.

She ascertained he was still at home, so she wrote him a note, saying she trusted he would make it a point to come to her; she had to speak to him on a subject that admitted of no delay, and she begged he would not fail.

In half-an-hour, a note came from Mrs. Graham. She was very sorry David had gone out, but as soon as he returned, her note should be given to him. She hoped if it was anything she could do, that Hilda would send again; at any rate, she would call during the afternoon.

Now, she knew not what she could do. She could not see David, and Walter was gone, and she did not know when she was to see him again, for Sir William was in the room when he left, so she had no opportunity of asking him. She felt an utter feeling of despair taking possession of her; she was so alone—and yet with so many to care for her, and so many to protect her, not one to save her from this dreadful sacrifice.

What was the use now to her of lovers, or friends? They were worse than useless. She would have been better off had she stood alone in the world, poor, unbefriended, uncared for.

She had built all her hopes on Walter, and yet, though she had told him all, though she had told him plainly enough he had been the cause of her hatred to David, though she had told him it was her love for him caused her to revolt from the thought of marrying her cousin, or any other man. Still, he had left without any more comfort than a few words of sympathy, and a suggestion that she should found her only hope on David's generosity, a particle of which he knew did not exist in David's composition.

At the same time, there was nothing to reproach him with. What was it she expected from him? Not that he should marry her himself, for that she never thought of till she had told him everything, and then she determined to refuse doing so if he should have proposed it. But she had raised him, in her own heart, to the pinnacle of all that

was high-souled, high-minded, and honour-
able. Her faith in him was perfect, and it
was that faith that made her feel she could
implicitly trust him, and that by what he
said, she would abide.

But she did not know that within the re-
cesses of her heart there was an equally firm
belief in his love for her, and that he would
never let her marry her cousin, or any one
but himself.

If, without alluding to himself, he had told
her to be steadfast and firm in refusing Lady
Fordyce's wish, at the cost of her dying
aunt's anger or sorrow, she would have done
it, and she would have been satisfied, because
she had followed his advice. But this he
had not done. He had left her but one
loophole, and that once closed, he told her he
saw no other hope.

She thought of her mother. It was rarely

that it occurred to her to go to her in any difficulty, they were so little like mother and daughter; but Hilda now remembered that she was her mother, and that mothers sometimes will do for their children what no other relation—however fond they may be —will.

She would go to her, and see what could be done through her means. She was not long in getting herself ready when she had once made up her mind. She went into her aunt to tell her she was going; and Mrs. Phillips, who was still there, requested her aunt would desire one of the servants to go with her, as it was not right for her to be driving about in cabs by herself.

Matilda fancied Hilda might be going to meet Wentworth, and felt delighted with herself for being so discerning; but as Hilda informed her that Strange was ready to accompany her, there was nothing more to be said.

When Hilda reached Kensington, she began to fear Arthur's being at home, as he very often was on Saturdays, and she felt half inclined to return, but it was too momentous a point to be given up for such a mere *contretemps* as that would be, and so she gathered up her courage to face him too with her tale and appeal, if necessary. She was, however, spared that, for her mother told her Arthur was gone down to Brighton till Monday. He had not been well for two or three days, and he hoped the change would do him good.

"I am glad he is not here, Mamma, for I have come to talk to you. I am in a great deal of sorrow; and I think if I tell you all about it, you will be able to help me."

Mrs. Chichester was so unused to Hilda

coming to her in this sort of way, that she was perplexed and amazed beyond all measure. Whenever in any little difficulty before, Hilda had naturally gone for the remedy to her aunt; neither in joy nor sorrow had she ever made a confidant of her mother. There could be no blame attached to her for it—it was the result of circumstances only; but Mrs. Chichester had not seen it in that light. She was her child, and as such, she had expected much more in every way.

Up to three or four years old she had been her mother's idol, and she had lavished more fondness on her than on both her other children together. It was her great love for her that had given her strength to part from her, because it was for the child's good. But she had not had the sense to know, that it was impossible Hilda should grow up with the same unbounded love for her, there had existed when a mere infant; and this she resented to Hilda, not in words or deeds, but in feeling. She no longer loved her as she had done. She still loved the memory of her little darling ; but the Hilda of seventeen was not the Hilda of four. It was, therefore, with no very great warmth that Mrs. Chichester begged her daughter to tell her how she could help her.

"Have you seen my aunt since—let me see, when was it ?   Oh, only yesterday afternoon.   Of course you've not, but the time seems so long to me; it seems as if I had passed through years instead of hours !" and she looked so, her face was so sad and pale, and her eyes seemed heavy with sorrow. "You know, mamma, that that idea of my marrying David has still gone on existing in the minds of all who were at Burwood at the time it was suggested, but in my own ;

and from the time of my coming to town till the other night, when Arthur spoke to me about it, I have scarcely given the matter a thought. But, mamma, it is not only that —they look on it as an engagement; but my aunt wishes me to marry him immediately—and, oh ! I feel as if the very thought would make me go mad ! It won't kill me —I wish it would."

She stopped; it seemed as if the words she had uttered were enough to kill her, her whole frame shook with agony; it seemed as if the poor child must soon sink beneath such repeated bursts of anguish, if they were not stopped. She got up, and threw herself on her knees before her mother; and looking up, with such a piteous heart-broken countenance, said to her in a voice that would have even made David's heart relent had he seen her—

"Mother, save me! you know not the agony I have endured here," and she pressed her hand to her heart. " I feel as if it must break," and her head fell on her mother's lap, her breast heaving with suppressed sobs.

Mrs. Chichester was weeping; she could not have witnessed such a burst of grief un-moved, had it been any one she was indif-ferent to, but in her own child, the same— yes, she felt it now—the same she had so idolized, it roused all the mother's fondest sympathies within her.

"My poor, darling child! What can I do for you? If I can save you, God knows I will. But get up, Hilda, don't kneel to me; there is but one Being you should kneel to, and He can help you and guide with a strong hand and firm arm, that will never fail you."

Her mother tried to raise her, but she would not move.

" No, let me stay so," she replied, " whilst I tell you all." She raised her head; there were no tears in her eyes—she could not weep; it would have been better if she could. She took her mother's hand in her's. " I cannot marry David, because—because I love some one else," and her eyes fell; it was not that she was ashamed of her love for Wentworth—far from it; she was proud of it. She was proud of him and his love for her; but she that moment remembered his cautioning her never to mention it to any one, and she had now gone contrary to his advice and wishes. She would have given worlds to have unsaid it, but that was impossible. She had not yet betrayed who it was, and she would not.

" Poor Hilda ! poor child ! Have you told

your aunt this, and does she yet desire to see you David's wife? Say, and tell me all a little more clearly, for it seems to me impossible she could desire it under such circumstances."

"No, no, I have not told her; I would not tell her for anything on earth," eagerly replied Hilda. "Mr. Hancock told my uncle, last night, he knew not, from hour to hour, how long she might live. She is free from pain now; and he always said when that should be the case, her end would be very near, and any sudden shock or excitement might kill her at once."

"When did this idea first enter her head?" asked Mrs. Chichester.

"She only told me last night. I don't know how long she had thought of it. Mrs. Graham was present."

"And what passed between you?"

Mrs. Chichester found it difficult, now that her daughter was a little calmer, to get her to tell her what the facts really were, and she feared a renewal of her late violent grief.

"She told me she wished it to be on Monday morning in her own room, that she might witness it; and when I told her it was impossible, she said a great deal of all she had done for me—how she had loved me, and would I be the cause of her dying miserable, unhappy, by refusing her last request, and then, mamma, I promised. I have scarcely seen her since. I saw Mrs. Graham afterwards, and I appealed to her to save her own son from the misery that would ensue; and, mamma, she said she could not, that David loved me, and would not consent to the marriage being broken off. And I know," said Hilda, rising and standing before

her mother, "I know he hates me, as I hate
m. His reason for wishing to sacrifice
himself as well as me, I cannot imagine.
But if I am forced to marry him, I will tell
him I hate him, that I will not live with
him, that I will be no wife to him. That
he must abide by the result if he will not go
hand in hand with me to prevent this dreadful mockery of a marriage. No blessing
could attend vows uttered in falsehood. God
help me, what can I do?"

Her anger soon subsided, it was but for
the moment as she thought of David, but
with the recollection of Walter her sorrow
again returned. She sank down on a chair
by her mother.

"I thought of appealing to himself," she
continued, "to tell him I was not fit for
his wife. I sent a message asking to see
him, but he sent me an excuse; I then

wrote, and Mrs. Graham answered that he was gone out. Oh, mamma, is there nothing I can do, is there nothing that will save me, but perhaps killing my poor aunt, and if she did die I should never be happy again. Will you see David—will you speak to my aunt, perhaps it would make her alter her mind. Why has she fixed her heart on what will be such misery to me? Oh, that I could die instead; do you believe me, mamma?" she asked, in a calm voice, " that I would rather be laid in my grave, than marry that man."

"You must not talk so, Hilda. Remember always, that whatever does befal us is from God, it is not chance, it is His will; it is by His hand the blow comes, and it is always for our good. If it be His will that you become David Graham's wife, feel that no human aid could have saved you, no circumstances could have altered it, that it was decreed by Him for your good, and you will not look at it in the resentful bitter way you now see it in. If God thought it better for you to die, you would die; but if He sees differently, you must submit to His will, and if you do not feel submission, pray for it. It will come, he never refuses balm to the wounded."

"All 1 could pray for now," said Hilda sorrowfully, "would be to be spared this misery, I could not pray for anything else, it would seem a mockery. But cannot you do anything for me? Will you not go and see my aunt."

" Yes, I will ; but, Hilda, remember, unless you let me tell your aunt what you have just owned to me, how can I hope to influence her. I shall never have anything to argue on."

"You must not tell her, mamma," replied Hilda in a low subdued voice, "I ought not to have told you."

"Ought not, and why Hilda; if the one you love tells you that, if he would try to make you hide your love from those most interested in you, as if it were a disgrace or a crime, he is not worthy of the pure and holy love that alone can enter a girl's heart at your age."

"You are wrong," replied Hilda, with something of haughtiness in her tone, that her mother had often heard and felt with pain, when she addressed her so.

"If I am wrong, Hilda," replied her mother mildly, "I am glad of it. But who is it, can you not tell me who has gained your heart in this manner, without any person belonging to you knowing it?"

"No, I cannot," she answered sadly.

Mrs. Chichester at first had thought rightly that it was Mr. Wentworth, but now that
Hilda refused to say more about it, she suspected it must be some one else. But she
could not imagine who. Why should she
not be able to tell? Was she ashamed of
it? Could it be a love that she dared not
own? The idea was preposterous, but having
taken root, she could not pull it out. · She
wondered whether it could be possible that
Lady Fordyce knew, and so to save her from
any greater misery, was insisting on this
unhappy marriage. If so, that explained her
conduct; and how was she to act? How help
her child, perhaps to shame and ruin. She
would try once more what she could say to
obtain Hilda's entire confidence, and if she
failed she must leave it all in Higher hands.

" If you will not tell me anything more
about this attachment, Hilda, how can I

argue for you either to David or your aunt.
Tell me, I will keep your secret ; but let me
have it in my power to say I have good and
sufficient reasons for thinking the marriage
should not take place.   But if you do not
give me that power, I have no arguments
left.   It will be simply this.   Six months
ago you consented to marry your cousin, you
raise no objections, you say nothing about
not liking him, till your aunt, on her death-
bed, anxious to see you with a home of your
own, and a husband who will be a guide and
protector to you, and to whom she has promised you—asks you to fulfil your part
of the contract, and then without giving any
reason, any cause, you say you cannot.   It
would be folly· in me to go to her without
any other excuse than what every one would
call a foolish, girlish objection.   Why not
long since have spoken about it—have told

her you had changed your opinion of David, that you could no longer think of marrying him."

"I did," she replied, " the very day that my aunt met with her fatal accident; but even then she made me promise before she went out that I would do what she wished on the subject; she spoke to me in that sort of way that I could not help promising. She cried and said how she loved me, and then I felt for her sake I could do it. But when I think of it calmly—at least not calmly, for that is impossible—but when I try to realize it, it makes me shrink from the bare thought. Try, mamma, what your speaking to her will do, or David. I really think if you were to speak to him, it would prove to him the insane act it will be. Will you come with me now, for I must go back. I left Matilda there, but she is gone by this time, and my aunt alone, for my uncle went out before I did."

"I will go, Hilda, but I hope little; you give me a hard battle to fight and no weapons to defend myself with."

"I cannot, mamma—I dare not," she replied with firmness, but sadly.

"Well, then, I must do what I can without, but expect nothing, for I feel you will be disappointed if you do."

Mrs. Chichester went with her daughter, and being one of those people rarely met who think the truth the shortest way to arrive at an understanding, told Lady Fordyce she had come to try and dissuade her from urging Hilda to marry David with her present feelings. But Mrs. Graham had so well hidden all her objections under a thick coating of her own manufacture, that Lady Fordyce was now no longer clear-

sighted enough to see those offered by her
sister-in-law. She combated them, as Mrs.
Graham had done her's. She warded off,
by Mrs. Graham's own words to herself,
every blow from Mrs. Chichester's blun
argument; and she rose to take leave, nearly
persuaded that, though Hilda thought differently, the best and most prudent thing
that could happen to her, would be to become
David's wife.

She went to see Hilda before going back.
She told her it was as she expected it would
be—a fruitless effort she had made, and the
only comfort or hope she could give her was
a very sad one; and that was, she thought
it more than probable her aunt would not
live till Monday morning.

It was a mournful reflection for poor Hilda
to hear, that her only escape lay in her aunt's
death. Must she, then, resign herself to the

prospect of becoming the wife of a man she hated, in less than forty-eight hours, if her aunt should live that time. No, she could not, it was utterly impossible. She would not think of it any more, it only made her unfit for all her daily duties. She would do as her mother bade her—she would pray. And in her own room she fell on her knees, and implored God's hand to stay the blow that was hanging over her. She prayed fervently, but passionately. She implored His blessing on Wentworth, and His guiding influence to lead them to do what was right. She could not help coupling herself with him; he was her all—the dearest being in life to her; and she could not and would not give up hope, that yet she might be his own, his very own, in the sight of man as well as in the sight of God, for she felt as if in the sight of God she was his, heart and soul.

She was a little calmer after this, and she went to her aunt's room to sit by her the rest of the day, or till some one should come in and take her place. Lady Fordyce was sleeping—it might have been the sleep of death, it was so still. Hilda took a book and tried to read. She read several pages without knowing the name of the book, or what it was about, so she fell again into a train of thought that brought her back to all her misery and all her sorrow. The tears unconsciously fell, one by one, from her large blue eyes down her pale cheeks, but they were not tears of relief, they were like drops being drawn from her—hot, burning tears, that came without the convulsive sensation of weeping.

Mr. Hancock came in. He would not disturb Lady Fordyce. He asked Hilda some questions and shook his head. A thought suddenly struck her, and she asked him whether anything that affected her nerves, would be likely to be injurious under her present circumstances.

" Certainly, my dear young lady, I believe the poor sufferer's hours are now but few, and they will be quiet and free from pain, but any sudden shock or fright, would reduce the hours to minutes, perhaps to seconds. You must keep her free from every excitement, and let her have anything she likes— anything she asks, for nothing can harm her now in that way."

Poor Hilda, it is true, she had built no hope on Mr. Hancock, because till she saw him she did not think about it; but for the moment when to ask the question occurred to her, hope revived, to be dashed entirely down again. He went, and she returned to her chair, her aunt still sleeping; and so they

remained, hour after hour till, the sun began
to set, and her hopes of being saved gradually lessened, till they became little more
than a shadow. Lady Fordyce's maid came
in, and told her Lord Borton was down stairs
and wished to speak to her. The noise
roused her aunt. She opened her eyes and
looked vacantly around.

"It is not Monday morning yet," she
inquired, and then closed her eyes again.

"No, milady," replied the servant, "this
is Saturday evening."

"I am going down for a few minutes,
auntie, and I shall be back again," said Hilda,
but Lady Fordyce made no reply.

Lord Borton was standing with his back
to the door as she went in; he did not hear
her, so she had to speak before he turned
round.

"It is very kind of you to have called so

frequently, Lord Borton ; my aunt has once or twice expressed herself so gratified by the numerous friends who have so often inquired for her."

He started round at the first tone of her voice, and held out his hand, which she took without embarrassment or shyness ; she was too much occupied with her own thoughts to notice the strange expression in his face, which, though boyish and fair, was very handsome.

" How is Lady Fordyce?" he asked, still holding her hand, but he continued before she had time to answer him, " my visit to-day is to you. I want very much to speak to you—to ask you a question."

" Won't you sit down?" she said, withdrawing her hand with some difficulty. " What question do you wish me to answer ?"

" How shockingly ill you are looking, Miss Chichester," he said, paying no attention to what she had said. "It's a confounded shame—I believe it's true—and she will die of a broken heart." And the young man walked about the room as if he were greatly agitated. Hilda could not understand him. She sat quietly till he chose to explain himself; she was too indifferent to care to exert herself in order to find out what was the matter. "Is it true, Miss Chichester, is it true that they are going to marry you against your will to that thick-headed, yellow-faced Scotch devil? There, you don't answer—of course, it's true. I knew that the moment I saw your face. You don't like him, I know—you can't like such an ill-bred, uncouth monster! Now, listen to me," and he stood before her, and drew himself up to his full height. "Don't be offended if I speak plainly or say anything disagreeable, because I don't mean,—you know I wouldn't offend you for the world! They want you married to him, because they think he's rich and you've no fortune; and when your aunt is dead, perhaps you won't have so much going out, or so many opportunities of marrying, and all that sort of thing. I've got money, and a stupid title as well, which some people think a great deal of; but, besides them, I've got a heart to offer—a heart that does, and will continue to love you with truth and sincerity. People call me a boy, and all that sort of thing; but if I am, I feel like a man, and I feel as if I could grind that lubberly Graham to powder, for his impudence in daring to think of marrying you, with an ossified heart and an empty head. Now, Miss Chichester, look up a moment, and tell me whether you could not

like me better than that white-faced scoundrel,
and if so, if you won't have me? I can
marry you on Monday morning, as well as
he can, so they need not be disappointed on
that score; and I will stake all my fortune
that you shall never have cause, through me,
to repent the step."

He stopped, not because he had not more
to say, but to get breath to say it with.
Hilda did think she should be happier with
him than with David; she did think that had
it been him instead, she should not have felt
that abhorrence she did to the other; but she
thought of Walter—what would he say, what
would he think? No, she dare not do it.
Walter would say that if she were able to
persuade her aunt to consent to her marriage
with another man, she surely could have
persuaded her to defer it altogether. And
yet something within her said Walter had no

right to such consideration, but she crushed
the voice within her, she could not let it
affect her.

" Who told you this ?" she asked.

" I heard it at the club just now. The
fool himself had been there, he had just been
to procure a special licence, so that the
ceremony might be performed here in the
house. But don't let's talk of it or
him. Why should you ; you don't like
the man, do you ?" he suddenly asked, rather
alarmed.

" You deserve a frank answer in return for
your generous kindness. I do not like him,
but I fear there is little hope for me to escape
the marriage. I could not accept your offer,
Lord Borton, were he quite out of the question ; but I nevertheless thank you from my
heart for your sympathy, I thank you for
teaching me that there is yet something

worth having even in this world; for from
this day I shall value and hope to keep your
friendship and esteem." Her voice quivered,
and the dilated nostrils and trembling lips
showed the struggle she had to command
herself.

" My friendship ! you know well enough
you won't care a straw for that in a few
weeks, or perhaps days; but if you were my
wife, you might learn to like me a little, and
if you found you could not be happy with
me, I would leave you; you should be free to
come and go, as you most liked, I would
never interfere in anything you ever wished
to do. I am afraid you think me too young,
you look upon me as a boy, and you think
you could not look up to me. And yet I
feel my arm strong enough, and my heart
brave enough to shield you and guard you
from any danger that could come near you.

There is nothing like an honest love to make
a man of one, and I know I love you, because
I feel I could give up my own happiness, if
it could make up yours. Don't send me
away without a hope; tell me, I may come
to-morrow, and let me go now and talk to
Sir William Fordyce about it."

"You do not know, Lord Borton," said
Hilda, "how it pains me to hear you speak
so, for I feel and know I am refusing a
brighter lot than mine can ever be as the
wife of Mr. Graham. I tell you candidly
that I do not love you, but I like and esteem
you, and I could be very happy with you,
and perhaps in time love you as you deserve;
but it cannot be, I dare not give you hope,
for it would be false. You must forget you
have ever spoken to me on such a subject,
and you will soon meet one more worthy of
your love than I am, and you are sure to meet

with a return.   Think of me only as a sister, and let me think of you and regard you as a brother."

Lord Borton turned his face away for a moment, he was not ashamed of the tears that were in his eyes, but he did not wish to pain Hilda by letting her see them.

She rose up and held out her hand. "Whatever my fate may be," she said, "be sure of this, that I shall never forget to-day, or that I have found a friend I shall ever think of with pleasure.   We must part now, but God only knows whether we may meet again.   Perhaps it will be better we should not."

"God bless you, Hilda, dear Hilda, let me call you so for the first and last time.   If ever you should want a friend, one you may trust as a brother, you will let me be of use to you if I can.   Promise me this."

" I will," she replied. He pressed his lips to her hand, and rushed out of the room.

It is strange how perverse human nature is ; why could Hilda not have been satisfied with the honest manly love of poor Lord Borton. He said what was very true, if he was boyish in some things, his affection for her had made him man enough to suffer deeply at its rejection. But she could not, with her deep-rooted love for Walter, even voluntarily consent to become the wife of any other man. Had she been asked the simple question, which will you marry, Lord Borton or Mr. Graham ? she would have replied without hesitation, the former; but if left the option of refusing altogether, she would have done so.

She thought she was doing right in dismissing him under her present circumstances, for she felt sure, had she done otherwise, she would some time or other have repented. She felt very very angry at David having spoken about their marriage; it seemed to make it more difficult for her to bear. She thought from the manner Lord Borton had spoken to her about it, that he must have made a kind of boast of it; and if he was disengaged enough to go to his club, why could he not have found time to see her.. Mrs. Graham, too, had abstained from coming, they all seemed leagued together to force her down the precipice, and she felt alone she had not power to withstand them. If Walter had stood by her, her courage would never have forsaken her; but as he failed, so did everything else.

CHAPTER VIII.

WALTER WENTWORTH, after he had seen
Sir William's lawyer, and done what he had
requested, returned to town, and went to Mr.
Munro's lodgings, hoping to find him in.
But he was out. The servant, however, said
he expected him very soon, so Walter waited
and consoled himself with a cigar. He had
had no time to think since he had left Park
Lane in the morning, nor had he had the
inclination for it; it was disagreeable, and

made him feel ill at ease with himself, so he kept walking away from his thoughts as much as possible.

But now that he was sitting still, with a cigar to encourage them, they became stronger than himself, and would intrude themselves whether he would or no. They were unwelcome companions, but this time they were not to be got rid of. The truth was, he could not divest himself of the feeling that he had sneaked out of the affair in rather a selfish, cowardly manner. He had, in a clever, lawyer-like way of doing things, taken great care of himself, so that he could in no way be implicated, or called on to explain what he had intended doing, and he had left Hilda to bear the whole weight of misery alone.

He knew quite well, as things stood, there was no necessity for his returning to Park

Lane till after the dreaded Monday, and yet, he asked himself, could he let all the next day pass without going near her? Perhaps, if he did, he might never see her again; never hear her tell him how she loved him. He liked so hearing her tell him that, he never wearied of it.

He was by no means pleased with himself, and he was very glad when Mr. Munro walked in.

"Holloa, Wentworth, you here! What do you want?—and smoking, too! By Jove, what a fellow you are for a cigar, your inside must be a perfect chimney! Well, old fellow, you look down in the mouth. What's wrong with you?"

"I am in a confounded mess, and I don't see my way either out of it, or into it."

"Is it anything to do with the Fordyces? I heard at the club just now about a marriage being got up, not in wedding, but dying haste, between your little girl and that booby, Graham. I pity her, poor little thing!"

"You don't mean to say they are talking about it at the club? They didn't name me, did they?"

"No, I heard nothing about you; but Borton was there, and cursing Graham quite loud enough for him to have heard, if he had not been too much of an antiduelist to care to pick a quarrel with a hot-headed, love-sick boy, for I fancy the lordly stripling would be silly enough to place his hand and his fortune at pretty Hilda Chichester's feet."

"Oh, stop, Munro, for pity's sake don't go on with any more of that trash. Borton no more thought of her than you did. But I must tell you what has occurred, and then tell me what you would do were you in my place."

Walter then told him all that had passed between him and Hilda in the morning.

" It's an ugly business, Walter, and I am sorry you did not do what I begged you some time since, and that was, to leave her alone. You did not want to marry, and you must have known something of this sort would happen sooner or later, if you did not yourself come forward. However, it's done now, mischief and all, and it can't be worse. You need not hope that Graham will held out a finger to stop the marriage; from the way he spoke just now, I'm convinced he is anxious about it, though I don't believe in a particle of love being able to exist in such a being. And so, unless the old lady dies, there is no escape for the poor girl. I'm sorry for her; there was something very natural and taking in her, though her beauty was not so startling to me as to some men I've heard discuss her. I know but one thing you can do," he said, turning round and facing Walter, " and that is, write to her and tell her you fear there is no escape for her, that under such circumstances, your absence will be better than that she should keep feeling you were near to her; and therefore, by the time she receives the letter, you will have gone abroad till all is over. Of course, say anything you can that will comfort her; you may as well gild the pill, she will find it bitter enough to swallow."

Walter took his cigar out of his mouth, and whilst he was knocking off the ash, said, " I don't quite like writing, it's a dangerous thing to do. Whatever is put down in black and white can always be brought against you."

"But my good fellow," said Munro, a little put out by Walter's continued thought of self, "what harm can anything you write do you? You are not afraid of that thick Scotchman, I suppose? And you can't well leave the girl without one word, after having wrung her heart till, I suppose, it is nearly crushed. Remember, you sought her, you paid her constant and marked attention, you singled her out from every other girl in London to dance with, when no one scarcely ever saw you dance before. You make her confess she loves you ; you ask her to continue to do so ; you tell her to trust you, and it appears she trusted to you as she would to a rock, and she learns, when too late, she has been leaning against a sand-hill. No, don't treat her as. you would any woman who had known the world and its ways, or a woman who could trifle with a man's heart. Think for a moment of her own unselfish conduct; of her perfect, implicit faith in you; think of her youth, the long life before her that you have blighted for ever, for had you never crossed her path, she would have had a very different fate.   It is your duty now to do all you can to alleviate the misery she has before her. Let her know you can and do feel for her. It seems to me that is the very least you can do.   But don't see her; you know yourself that will but increase the evil.   If you feel that you cannot, or will not, by offering to marry her yourself, save her from becoming the wife of that idiot—then, as long as you live, you ought never to meet her again, for, depend upon it, as long as she lives, she will continue to love you."

Walter was by no means pleased at the tone in which Munro spoke to him in; and he, probably, was the only man who would have dared to speak in so open a manner. He had not said half he could have said, and felt inclined to say, but he knew Walter's disposition and temper too well, to risk losing his friend by telling unpleasant truths, that he feared would fall on barren ground, there being no good to result from it; perhaps he was wise to stop where he did.

" I think the plan of going away, good," said Walter, "and I can do that easily enough, but I don't quite like writing and telling her I am going on purpose, I would much rather some sudden business called me away."

" She would not believe it if you wrote a hundred times," replied Munro, " and for Heaven's sake, try and keep to the truth as much as possible; what use is there in going out of the way to tell a lie. If she found it out, I think she would, perhaps, be cured of her passion for you.   For if I ever read a countenance right in my life, I am sure it was hers, when I ˉsaid truth was written in every line of it.   Come, Wentworth, don't lose time, but be off; write your letter, leave it to be sent as soon as you are started, which you had better do as soon as you can, and cross over to Boulogne by to-night's boat."

" Well, as I must do something, I suppose I may as well do that.   But it seems almost an unkind act towards old Fordyce, for really he lately has appeared to look to me to do everything for him, and he will think it so marvellous for me suddenly to disappear without rhyme or reason."

" That's easily arranged," said Munro, " write him a line, saying private affairs of some importance require your absence for a few days. To him that will be true, but to her it would have been false."

Munro was not a bad fellow at heart, though his actions perhaps at times might have been rather doubtful. He had a great love of truth, and had he by thoughtlessness, or vanity, placed himself in Walter Wentworth's position, he would have done all in his power to repair the injury, for he was not naturally selfish.

Walter walked leisurely towards his lodgings; he was still not decided what he should do, his sense told him that he ought not to see Hilda again, but he longed to do so, and once having allowed the wish to gain sufficient strength to make him doubt, he soon decided to call first in Park Lane. He had a good excuse, by telling Sir William he had done his bequest. So he turned his

steps towards it, his longing to see Hilda
increasing as he neared her home.

He first asked if Sir William was within,
and hearing he was not, asked for Miss Chichester; but she, too, was out, had just gone,
did not know how long she would be, was
not walking, had gone in a cab. Then there
was no use in his waiting, he supposed it
was fated he was not to see her.

Ile retraced his steps, and felt sadder than
he liked, or was pleasant to him. He tried
to shake it off, but it would not do, her pale
sad face would rise before him, appealing to
him to advise how she could be saved; and
he found himself slinking away out of the
country to avoid helping her in her sorrow.
What a broken reed she had leant on.

What mist could have been before her
eyes when she looked up at his handsome
countenance, and saw nothing there but truth

and honour. What blinded her judgment when he told her she must never speak of their love, as it might prevent their meeting if her family suspected it, and she thought it was for her and on her account he was so careful, so cautious? Oh, blind indeed have you been, poor Hilda; but you are not the first, nor will you be the last. Human beings, are morally, what puppies are physically, born blind, only the latter soon receive their sight, whereas the former have their eyes torn open by the corruption and wickedness of the world. It is a violent and painful operation, but all have to undergo it alike, and so no one is pitied or sympathized with; it is a matter of course.

Happy are those who remain the longest in their blind existence; they have so much more of earthly happiness to enjoy, so much longer of the belief in human excellence to

revel in, but it must come at last, unless
death snatches us away whilst we are in our
first youth, and enviable are those whom
God takes away from the sorrows to come.

Hilda and Sir William passed a dismal
evening together. Lady Fordyce was so
still, she scarcely seemed to breathe; she
was not asleep, but as she never spoke, they
feared disturbing her. There was a restraint
between them that neither had felt before.
Hilda had become very fond of her uncle,
but she could not confide in him, and he felt
she had in some way not acted openly about
Walter Wentworth. Both were glad when
bed-time came to release them. There was
no rest though for Hilda, she could not sleep.
She could not even make up her mind to lie
on her bed. At about twelve o'clock she
went very softly into her aunt's room. She
told the nurse who had roused up on her

going in, that she could go to bed, as she meant to sit by her aunt; the woman was glad enough, and went without requiring much pressing.

Hilda took her chair and placed it close by the bed, she sat down, and so passed the night, her eyes closed, but she never lost consciousness for one moment. Beyond the ticking of the clock there was no sound in the room; her aunt never once moved the whole night; the stillness was oppressive to her, she felt nervous, she every now and then got up and put her hand before Lady Fordyce's mouth, that she might feel she breathed.

She longed for morning; she went to the window and stood waiting for an hour for the first streak of dawn, and when it gradually broke, when light came slowly and imperceptibly, when she began to see first

one object and then another, she longed
again for the blackness of night to hide and
blot out that beautiful world, that to her
was so replete with anguish and sorrow.

She put out the light that was burning in
the room.   Nothing is so disagreeable as daylight and candle-light together, especially if
it happens to be the first light of day.   And
she went and sat at the window, and offered
up her morning prayers to her Heavenly
Father.   She knew not what to pray for or
against, her heart was too stricken down with
grief.   She only asked Him to bless her and
those dear to her, and lead her out of temptation and from evil.

At length she heard some movement in
the house ; she looked at the clock, it was
nearly seven, so she once more went to the
side of the bed, saw Lady Fordyce still quiet
and sleeping, and she went back to her room,

having called the nurse to take her place. At nine o'clock, when she went down to the breakfast-room, she saw a letter addressed to her in Walter's hand lying on the table at her place. Her hand trembled as she took it up; a throb of desponding hope for a moment rose in her breast; she felt a suffocating, choaking sensation in her throat; she was so glad, she happened to be alone, that her uncle was not down yet. She opened the letter and read,

" Saturday evening.

"I scarcely know, my dearest Hilda, how to address you, or say all I wish and feel about your sad position. If I could have alleviated it in any way by anything I could have done, you must know I would have done so; but I thought it all over, and I found it was impossible. I heard your

marriage openly spoken of to-day, and from
the tone Mr. Graham assumed, I fear the
plan I proposed of trying to get him to break
it off will fail.   I called this afternoon to see
you and take leave of you, for I am convinced my absence altogether for the present
will be better.   By the time this reaches you
I shall have left England, I could not have
remained near you, and not come to you.
You must try and bear up, dear Hilda; you
have a brave, strong heart, and God grant
you may yet have years of peace and happiness before you.   You must forget our love,
forget we were ever more to each other than
I hope and trust we may yet be in the future,
true and sincere friends.   I shall never forget
the happiness you were the means of my
enjoying, and I ever regret the circumstances
that denied me the power of claiming what I
should have so valued.   Farewell, may God

bless you, and give you strength to endure the trial before you.

"W. W."

Hilda held the letter tightly grasped in her hand, her eyes fixed on the words, her lips and face were as white as the table cloth near her. He was gone, that seemed the only point her mind could understand ; gone—left England—left her ! The very completeness of her despair roused her, she looked round the room again to see if she was alone, for she seemed as if she had forgotten for the moment where she was. She then read the letter once more. He told her to forget their love, to forget that they were anything but friends. Was this the man she had loved ; that she had pinned her whole life's happiness to ; that she had trusted as implicitly as she would an angel from heaven ; that she thought

VOL. III.   R

too good for her; to whom in her blind idola-
trous love she had confided every desire and hope
of her heart; that she had enshrined in her
breast, and worshiped as God does not permit
his creatures to worship each other. Was it
to be told by himself to forget him that she
had done all this? The scales were being
roughly and hardly removed from her eyes,
and she was beginning to see her false god
divested of his bright and glorious casing.
Her teeth were clenched together, her eyes
glistened unnaturally, and there was an
expression of pride and disdain in her face,
that had never crossed it before. Hilda
Chichester was suddenly changed from the
gentle, loving, confiding girl, to the hard,
suspicious, disappointed woman. She re-
solved she would forget him, but she would
not remember him as a friend. No, she
prayed to God to crush her love, if any still

remained, to make her forget him entirely and completely. He should never pity her, never think of her as a love-sick girl, she would conquer every feeling within her, that breathed of kindness towards him.

She would so control all her thoughts, that he should never cross her mind again; she would blot him out from her recollection as if she had never seen him, never known of his existence. Should their paths in life ever cross, she would meet him as a common stranger, she would show no pique, for fear he should think she had not forgiven him his cowardly unmanly conduct.

But the re-action soon came, the violence of her anger soon subsided, and Hilda once more the heart-broken but loving girl, gave vent to her uncontrolable anguish. It burst forth with such a bitter cry, that it was well none were near to hear it; her whole body seemed in agony, she shook and trembled like a tender plant in a heavy storm, and like it, seemed in danger of being destroyed. She tried to restrain her grief, but she could not, nature would take its course, and her tears had been stayed too long for the flood gates of her eyes, when once opened, not to have their full vent. It was better it should be so, for it would have killed had she continued much longer with her grief stifled and suppressed, as it had been of late. How long it continued she did not know, but when at length she felt the violence of it over, she hurried up to her own room. It was some time before she could overcome the hysterical sobs that followed, she laid on her bed for a few moments, and then used all her endeavours to remove the traces from her face.

But that was not so easily done; she was startled by her own appearance; she could

scarcely recognize herself in the face reflected
before her; her cheeks seemed sunken, her
eyes swelled, and a black ring round each of
them, the veins in her forehead starting, her
lips parched and dry. It was useless trying
to hide all these signs of the suffering she
had gone through, so she determined to go
down; if she refused, and her uncle came to
her, it would be worse. She still held
Walter's letter in her hand; she put it in her
desk and locked it up, she did not dare to
read it again, there was no need, for every
word seemed written in letters of fire on her
brain.

Sir William was in the room when his
niece returned, she said good morning as
usual. He was reading a letter, so he did
not notice her, but presently he handed it to
her to read, and then watched her countenance.
He made no remark till she had finished it.

The words were simple enough, merely saying private and urgent business took him from town for a few days, and so excusing himself from being able to call till his return; but it was a long time before she could decipher them, they seemed to swim before her. But at last she finished it, and handed it back to her uncle. She could not trust herself to speak, she knew she could not command her voice.

"Did you know this, Hilda?" asked Sir William; but she could not reply.

"I have not spoken to you on this subject, or about this strange sudden wish of your aunt's, because you seemed to avoid it with me. I thought you were attached to Walter, and was pleased at it, for I like him; but when your aunt told me you had consented to marry David, I could not understand it. Now your miserable, unhappy looking face, and his going suddenly away, again mislead me. What is the mystery, what makes you look so broken-hearted? If it is that you have refused Walter in order to gratify your aunt, and that you love him, I think you are not only foolish, but very very wrong; I don't believe you like David, and therefore for a mistaken idea of duty, you will cause two people's future happiness to be destroyed as well as your own."

"Don't ask me any questions just now," sobbed Hilda, "for I feel as if I could not speak."

Sir William, who was never talkative or communicative himself, seemed to know and understand what she felt, and did as she asked him. It was not till much later in the day, that on Lady Fordyce sending for her, he again asked her whether it was not possible for her to explain to him the cause of her grief. If it was the prospect of marrying David only, he would see what could be done to put it off.

"It is too late now, dear uncle, you are very, very kind, but all must now go on as is arranged, and if it pleases God to spare my aunt till the morning I will marry David."

"Why, Hilda, what do you mean by too late? You don't like or esteem him, I know."

"Still, though that is true, I have but the one course to pursue; besides," she added, as if to give some weight to her argument, "Mr. Hancock told me anything that could worry or vex my poor aunt, or even excite her, would probably be her last moment, and I would not have that on my heart to save me even from this."

Lady Fordyce wanted to speak to her niece about her dress. She must wear white; she must be properly dressed, though it would be such a melancholy wedding.

"But it will make me so happy, my darling! I can think of nothing else. What dress can you wear, dear?"

Poor Hilda! must she even bring herself to think how she was to be decked for a ceremony, that was to dash from her every hope of future peace or rest.

"Don't look so sad, my child," continued Lady Fordyce, noticing her worn and weary looking face, "it is true that it is a sorrowful way of marrying, by the side of a death-bed; but when I am gone, you will soon be gay enough, you will soon forget the cause that made it so gloomy; and you have this to reward you, that I die in blessing you for making me so happy."

"Oh, auntie, if I could always hear you say that, I should indeed feel sufficiently re-

warded.   But don't think I am sad because
of the manner it is being done in, it is because—"

"Because what, dear?" asked Lady Fordyce, as Hilda hesitated.

"Because of the thought of parting with
you so soon and for ever," replied Hilda.

Foolish girl!   Was she trying to deceive
herself, or her aunt, or both?   It would not
have been too late then for her to have told
her the pure, unvarnished truth.   But she
was still under the influence of Walter's letter, and she acted under a wrong, mistaken
notion; the thought that if she now were to
succeed in breaking her marriage off with
David, Walter would think it was on his
account, made her firm in her determination
to drink her cup of sorrow to the very dregs.
Once an idea flashed across her.   Could she
not now marry Lord Borton?   She thought

if she could only have met him by chance again, and that he should allude to their conversation of yesterday, it might be. But then arose all the innumerable difficulties that would attend such a plan, and probably, might fail in the end. She began to feel it was her destiny to become David's wife, and there was no use in fighting against fate any longer. A few more hours, and all would be decided.

During the remainder of the day, numerous enquiries were made for Lady Fordyce, and several visitors who asked, were admitted; amongst the rest, old Lord and Lady Willesden. But Hilda had given orders to let no one in to her, and so she was saved answering all the questions she felt sure would shower down upon her, as no doubt every one had heard of what was going to take place.

She had received no answer from David to

her note, so it was evident he did not intend coming. But she did not need it now. If he came, she would say nothing, therefore she would rather be spared seeing him.

Nothing occurred during the remainder of the day, but a note coming from David for Lady Fordyce, telling her he had everything in readiness, and that at ten o'clock the following morning, the Rev. W. Davenport would be there to perform the ceremony.

Hilda and her uncle were both sitting in the room when she received it; she handed it first to her husband, and he, after reading it, gave it to Hilda. Not a remark was made by either of them.

On wishing her aunt good night, Hilda said, " You must not ask me to leave you, dear auntie, to-morrow, I must remain with you till you are taken from me by God's will."

"No, darling, we will not part till death parts us. I sometimes wish, Hilda, I might have been spared to see your happiness."

The poor girl shook her head mournfully.

"It is better as it is," she replied, and went away to pass another night in still more cruel torment than the previous one.

She could not, bitter as her feelings were, long for the morrow, for what a morrow would dawn for her. She could not say with Tennyson,

> "I hold it true, whate'er befal,
> I feel it when I sorrow most,
> 'Tis better to have loved and lost,
> Than never to have loved at all."

She would rather never have known what love was than suffered as she did now. Were they weighed in the scale, though her love was as pure and strong as human love could be, the sorrow she had endured would have weighed the balance heavily down.

Time, however, passes, whatever is happening, whether we are under the influence of pleasure or pain. It is fortunate it is so, for what may be a moment of agony to us, may be one of supreme felicity to another, and we should, without scruple to spare ourselves, deprive our fellow-creatures. What a world it would be if human beings were invested with more power than they have already. What tyrants we should be one to the other; how merciless we should be if we had the means allowed us; how little pity we should meet with, or give. For our hearts are evil by nature. The heart may know its own bitterness, but not its own wickedness. We know not how corrupt our nature is, till circumstances call our evil passions forth. There is very little good amongst the best of us, and that little exists only when we are young, and before we are corrupted and vitiated by the world's baseness and falsity.

But we have wandered far away from time and poor Hilda, whom the world was beginning to sully and tarnish, as it does every bright thing of God's creation. It is a thick, black, muddy pool, that all who go in it must come out of tainted and soiled, and the clearest brook can never entirely free one from its impurities.

Every hour of that night did Hilda hear strike by the church clock in the distance. The hours seemed to fly, and yet, God knows, they were sad enough ; but it was that they were drawing her nearer to a still more dreaded time than the present.

Towards morning, she fell into a heavy

sleep. It was so long since she had had rest, that noise did not disturb her, and her maid came in and out several times; but she slumbered on, unconscious of all.

At length, Strange, in despair, for it was nearly nine o'clock, went up and roused her by actual force. She told her Lady Fordyce was asking for her, that she appeared very excited and nervous, and frequently enquired if she were ready and dressed, and if she had a white dress on.

Hilda went in to see her aunt as soon as she got up, and told her she should be ready in time, and not to send for her again till they were wanting her.

Hilda then returned to her own room, dismissed Strange, and desired her not to disturb her till a quarter before ten. A little less than half an hour was all the time she had before her. But one short half hour.

She felt in a dream. Was it really possible that in so short a time she would have to perjure herself, soul and body, away? Could it be that in a few minutes she would have given David the right to command her love and obedience? The one she would give, but the other, never!

She knelt down to her God to pray for strength to carry her through — His blessing and forgiveness if she erred—His aid to guide her rightly in the future; she rose comforted and strengthened. Her mother came in presently; she came to fetch her. All was ready—all were waiting. Once more poor Hilda gave vent to a burst of grief, such as threatened completely to shatter her slight frame. Her mother tried to soothe and quiet her, but all in vain; it was not till a powerful restorative was given her that she became calm.

It was past the hour, and yet she was not ready. She had but her dress to put on, but nothing would induce her to wear white. She chose a black dress, and was obstinate in her determination to wear it. It was, indeed, the most appropriate; it seemed more in harmony with the whole scene. Sir William went to see if his niece was coming, for poor Lady Fordyce had twice murmured her name, and seemed restless and uneasy. Mr. Hancock was present and standing by her side, with his hand on her pulse, which he never removed till within five minutes before the conclusion of the ceremony.

Presently Hilda came in leaning on her uncle's arm, her mother following. She needed the support—she could hardly stand. There were between ten and twelve people in the room, and not one of them ever forgot the woe-stricken face of the poor young bride. None remarked her black dress, or the agony depicted in every feature of her beautiful face; even Mrs. Phillips felt her malicious tongue silenced for the time.

Hilda went up to her aunt's bed, and leaning over her, kissed her. The dying woman tried to speak, but could not. She raised her eyes, and with her finger pointed to where the rest of those present were standing. Hilda understood her and moved away. She had not seen David, though she felt he was there, and by the side of her. The clergyman began in a low, impressive voice, but not a word of the whole service reached her ears.

She never remembered anything of that terrible morning, but Mr. Hancock coming up to her, when she was standing as she thought alone in the room, and taking her hand in a tender, kind manner, led her to the side, and whispered to her that all was over. At first she could not comprehend what he meant, but she soon saw, by the rigid but placid look on her aunt's face, that her spirit had returned to God, who gave it. Then unconsciousness for a time happily deprived her of the power of fully realizing her position.

She fell across the bed fainting. She had seen no one in the room, and yet they had all been there, and all knew what she did not —that her sacrifice had been in vain, for Lady Fordyce had passed away before she knew her wishes were being fulfilled. She died too late to save her niece. One hour sooner, and what a different destiny might Hilda's have been.

" Guard her carefully," were Mr. Hancock's parting words to David, pointing to her lifeless form, " or you will soon have to sorrow over her too."

CONCLUSION.

Our task is nearly over; a very few more words, and all that remains to tell of Hilda Chichester's history will be told. Three months after the scene detailed in the last chapter, death mercifully terminated all Hilda's earthly sorrows. The shock and strain on her nerves had been too much; she never seemed to rally from the last struggle she had gone through just before her marriage. She seemed to have no disease, she never complained, she was quiet, and gentle, and grateful for any kindness, but she seemed gradually and rapidly sinking from day to day.

A month after her marriage, she went with her husband, and his father and mother, to Forestfern. David was kind to her in his way; it would have been impossible for him to have been otherwise, seeing her in the helpless state she was in. The next month of her life she had to be carried from her bed to the sofa.

Her mother had come down, and was with her till the last. She never alluded to her sorrow or the cause of it. She smiled when she spoke of her death—she looked forward to it with eagerness. There were none to grieve for her much; her mother would probably feel it most, but not as she would have done had they never been separated.

She passed from life to death, and on from
death to life everlasting without a struggle—
she slept like a young child!

As David stood over her, and thought of
the share he had wilfully taken in destroying
her life's whole happiness, and probably
causing her death, he felt remorseless sorrow
that made him a better man. He stooped
down, and kissed the white, cold brow of his
dead wife, and a hot, burning tear fell on her
lifeless cheek.

There was one other that did not belong
to that household, who heard with unfeigned
grief of the young bride's death, and that
was Lord Borton.   He mourned for her
more than as for a sister, for he loved her
still truly and sincerely.

Whether Walter Wentworth felt any con-
trition for the large share he had in her
death, I know not.   He must have known

and heard of it, but he shewed no signs of
grief; and within six months after, his marriage with the Dowager Lady Richman was
announced in the papers.

Mrs. Chichester went to live with her
brother—more to save him from an invasion
of the Phillips's than anything else.

Arthur was at Burwood as much as possible, and in due course of time Lucy Fenton
became Lucy Chichester. She was quite the
sort of wife for him, mild and yielding—no
opinion but his ; no wish to do anything but
his will. And so we trust their life may
so continue free from home sorrows and
vexations.

Frank is still in India, a gallant officer and
a good man. He never heard the particulars
of his sister's marriage, but her death was a
great blow to him, and the great inducement
for his wishing to leave India was gone ; but

we hope he may come before it is too late to be a stay and comfort to his mother, who is still living, though old now and somewhat infirm ; and may there yet be many merry, happy days at Burwood.

THE END.

LONDON :

Printed by A. Schulze, 13, Poland Street.

www.ingramcontent.com/pod-product-compliance
Lightning Source LLC
Chambersburg PA
CBHW020349030726
47496CB00007B/2074